About the author

Gary Barker is the founder of Promundo, an international organization that works in post-conflict Africa, Latin America, and in the Middle East to prevent violence. He is co-chair and co-founder of MenEngage and a member of the UN Secretary General's Men's Leaders Network to end violence against women. Gary Barker has been awarded an Ashoka Fellowship and an Open Society Fellowship for his research and activism. In 2015 he co-wrote the anti-war novel *The Afghan Vampires Book Club*, with Michael Kaufman. Gary Barker lives in Washington, D.C.

Mary of Kivu

Gary Barker

Mary of Kivu

World Editions

Published in Great Britain in 2016 by World Editions Ltd., London

www.worldeditions.org

Copyright © Gary Barker, 2016
Cover design Multitude
Image credit © Richard Mosse/Institute

The moral rights of the author have been asserted in accordance with the
Copyright, Designs and Patents Act 1988

British Library Cataloguing-in-Publication Data
A catalogue record for this book is available on request from
the British Library

ISBN 978-94-6238-005-9

Typeset in Minion Pro and Calibri

Distribution Europe (except the Netherlands and Belgium):
Turnaround Publisher Services, London
Distribution the Netherlands and Belgium: CB, Culemborg, the Netherlands

For all the Mary's in the Democratic Republic of Congo—
and everywhere else

IN THE BEGINNING

The man slowly pushes the woman in the wheelchair across the crumbled lava rock. He redoubles the force in his arms from time to time to keep the wheelchair moving. He bends his knees and his lower back to amass more strength. Occasionally he stops to catch his breath.

There are others on the street, this path they are on, the porous charcoal-gray-black path, remains from one of the most recent eruptions, more than ten years ago. Around us are makeshift houses built on the now hardened and long-since-cooled lava. But I seem to be the only one paying any attention to this man struggling to push the woman in the wheelchair.

It was during a stop in Goma, on the way to find Mary of Kivu, in the eastern part of the Democratic Republic of Congo, the place of 5 million war-related deaths and 500,000 women raped, numbers so round and so vague that we know no one has really been counting.

I distinctly recall the sound of walking on the lava path, the crunch, the coarseness of the gravel under my shoes, the feeling of it giving way and the more solid ground breaking through at uneven intervals.

The woman in the wheelchair is dressed in a blue and gold African wax print dress with a matching head wrap. The man pushing the wheelchair wears an oversized light blue dress shirt, untucked, and dress pants that look as worn as his non-descript black-gray shoes.

The wheelchair, a simpler version than is produced in this part of the world, gets stuck in a particularly gravelly part of the path, and the man struggles even more to push it. The woman laughs an openmouthed, happy-funny laugh and her eyes laugh along. She grips the armrests more firmly as the man—who, like her, could be forty or sixty, you can never tell here—leans down to apply more force. As he does, his legs slip on the lava gravel and he falls to his knees, his hands still on the grips on the back of the wheelchair. With that, the wheelchair slightly tilts its front wheels up. A wheelchair wheelie. Now he laughs too and her laugh intensifies.

The man, still smiling, gets to his feet to make another go at it, and as he does the woman turns her head slightly to the left and up so she can meet his eyes.

Their eyes engage for a few seconds, about as long as such outward displays of affection are considered acceptable here.

I had rarely seen moments like this between men and women in the heart of the conflicts in Africa, where I write and work. That is, until I found Mary. Or better to say it this way: until Mary found me.

ONE

It was Sam, agent for my books and editor of my magazine articles, who suggested I write an article about Mary of Kivu. He sent me links to two websites. One website showed naïf-style paintings of an African woman who appeared saint-like, healing and consoling villagers. On the paintings there were stenciled letters that said, in French and Swahili:

Mary of Kivu eats here.
Mary shops here.
Mary works here.
Mary studied here.

It was unlikely that Mary was present in so many places in the region given the ongoing conflict and how difficult travel is, but that was not the point.

On the other website there was a single photograph of the real-life Mary. In that picture, she was looking away from the camera and was slightly out of focus; perhaps she had just glared at the photographer and was turning away. The impression was a bit like a Bigfoot photo: you doubted it was real. Your eyes tried to make the photo clearer, tried to will it into focus. But to no avail.

* * *

'Keith, you should check it out. Try to find out more about her.'

It was one of those moments when mobile phone reception from New York to Kigali, Rwanda, which I used as base for traveling into eastern Congo, was exceptionally good; we could have been talking from down the street.

'Waste of time,' I told Sam.

'Might make for an interesting chapter between Mai Mai warlords and ex-*genocidaires*.'

'I've got plenty of backstory for the Congo book. I've been stuck in enough villages and military bases, getting it even when I don't want it. I've heard colonels swear they've seen women cured of cancer by the touch of a pastor's hands. Or that they've seen decomposing bodies come back to life. At first it's interesting. After a while only hardcore anthropologists care.'

'Maybe. But the big women's rights NGOs are posting her picture and I heard that the Vatican is sending someone to investigate. This one's getting around. No one's been able to interview her.'

'Okay. You want to call Ian at *The New Yorker* and ask if they'd be interested? If I got something good,' I said.

'Yeah. *Bonne chance*. Keep an open mind.'

* * *

The information Sam had was that Mary's village was on the north side of Lake Kivu, the Congolese side, some six or seven hours drive from Kigali, in the part of Congo where the conflict was active. He knew I would go; this is what I do.

Crossing the border into the Democratic Republic of Congo

from Rwanda is always an event. The paved road ends on the Rwandan side and the river of potholes and muddy roads starts on the Congolese side. The metal bar that is lifted for cars and trucks to pass is painted with neatly delineated stripes on the Rwandan side; on the Congolese side it is rusting and seems never to have been painted. The Rwandan soldiers are alert; they look like they would give chase. They scrutinize me and then they hand my documents back as if they have truly looked me over.

The Congolese soldiers give looks of indifference, or of anemia.

As I pass my passport to the Congolese border official, he waits a nearly discrete moment before he says, in French: What do you have for me? In spite of the chaos around us, the Congolese guards wear pressed uniforms, and take their version of protocol (which for some includes the expectation of the small favor, so as not to call it a bribe) seriously.

There are now two officials looking at my passport; there have not been many Americans, or *mzungus* of that matter, crossing here recently. *La violence*, they say. First they ask me for fifty dollars, then they reduce this to thirty dollars. Initially they will not take my hundred dollar bill. Then they won't take my Rwandan francs. Then they decide they need to see my vaccination card. Still they are reluctant. I show them my press card. More indifference.

At last I bring out a copy of my book on Joseph Kony and the Lord's Resistance Army. I have copies both in French and English; my picture is on the back cover.

'I'm a writer, a journalist,' I say again in French. 'Here is my most recent book.'

This gets their attention.

'Lord's Resistance Army ... They are horrible. That Kony. He is the worst,' one of the officials says.

As if there could be a contest, an Olympic event of mad men in Africa. Who invented bush wives first? Who is fastest at traumatizing twelve-year-old boys to become cold-blooded soldiers? Just what is the smallest child who can carry a semi-automatic weapon? Exactly what does it take to terrorize a village so that the residents don't dare return to claim the property that their families have farmed for centuries.

'Yes, Kony is evil,' I say. 'Very, very bad. I interviewed some of his commanders. They are frightening men.'

This gets movement.

I hear them telling their co-workers that I have written a book on the Lord's Resistance Army and that I have interviewed Kony's top men.

Then there is the familiar sound of the stamp coming down on the passport page, as if the exaggerated noise were an obligatory part of the process. There is the slow sliding of the passport to me through the window and the hanging onto it for just a few seconds longer than necessary. I have learned in these exchanges never to insist, nor to be in a hurry.

As I stepped into Congo, I thought for a moment of what my previous Congolese driver, who was ridiculously overqualified to be a driver, told me about these border crossings. He said that since the Great War (meaning the Great African War of the late 1990s), he now breathes a huge sigh of relief every time he comes to the Rwandan side. He told me: 'The Rwandans, they know how to manage things, to run a country and a military. They do not ask questions. They just follow orders and it works. Eh, but we, the Congolese, we know how to live and how to think. And how to argue. But we do not take orders. And so, *mon ami*, this is what you get.'

With my passport in hand, I was back on the road with my new driver, going to find Mary of Kivu. That meant stopping at *the* hospital, the one where the celebrities come to hug the women and then step back into their air-conditioned cars. The one that receives and repairs the destroyed bodies of women that the Great African War has produced.

I have a way of approaching these moments, and these interviews. I write down the details. I write them down in my head first and later I put them on paper.

I pay attention to the white lines painted around the rocks that ring each tree on the walkway to the hospital's main entrance. Or I might, as I had on a previous visit, observe the trousers the male orderly is wearing and wonder where the elegant but slightly excessively shiny polyester fabric came from. I complement the orderly on his trousers and he tells me that he bought them from a seamstress at the market. And I find time to go to the market and find her. On the way I stop to smell the smoked fish surrounded by flies.

I will find out that the old sewing machine the woman uses came from a missionary who was here a few years ago, and that this same *mzungu* woman came down with a difficult case of malaria and had to leave Congo. Then the Congolese seamstress will tell me that the missionary woman, who lives in a small town in Canada, sends her postcards, and the seamstress will tell me that she would like to write her back but the post office rarely works for outgoing mail and she doesn't have enough money for the postage. Then this woman will tell me about the pig farm that her husband has, but how he can't work as much as he used to because he was wounded and got an infected leg the last time the Mai Mai came through, and that the wound on his leg from the deep *panga* cut wouldn't heal and then the doctors taught them to use the sugar wound treatment.

I will ask about this sugar treatment, which I learn online is a new low-cost way to treat wounds, and I will include this in my article or a book chapter, and suddenly I have another element to my story. More importantly, in these details I have created a firewall between myself and the scope of human tragedy here—a firewall I need to continue doing this for a living.

And when I arrive at *the* hospital, I hope, above all, that they do not introduce me to the other *mzungus*. They are here to save these poor women, to raise money in 10k runs and to feel that they have done their part for social injustice. Or they spend more time on their blogs posting photos of this beautiful land than they do actually accomplishing anything and thus justifying their hardship pay. Or they have become so adrenaline-fazed from this work that they can function in no other place and in no other job. And they have become even more cynical than I am. Or they are running from something in their own lives, or perhaps looking for something in these women—fellow abused women to make sense of abuse they themselves suffered.

I must believe it all, believe that these intentions and motives are justifiable and that real improvement is possible, that lives can be saved. And I must, at the same time, believe none of it. It becomes easier to start with an assumption of mistrust. I assume they do the same of me. They're right to distrust my motives; I assume, therefore, I am right to distrust theirs.

* * *

The route to Mary's village takes us first on the unmarked lake road, the one that winds along the tiny fingers and coves and hills that surround the lake. There are patches of red earth being tilled, or sometimes eroding, along with the never-ending green fields, hills, and trees.

I see women tilling undulated plots of land while a man looks on—one man supervising ten or fifteen women. Beyond them are terraced hills that create a patchwork carpet of various shades of green. Then we see the unroasted, pallid coffee beans drying on white tarps in front of small warehouses built out of cinderblocks. The lake comes into view again, through patches of trees and bushes, framed as perfectly as it is in the photos in the blogs of aid workers.

I roll down the window. It is quiet outside. We are the only ones making noise. The air feels fertile and the temperature is spring-like today, as it is much of the year.

Further ahead, I see the edge of the lake again, and long, thin boats, laden with large white sacks of foodstuffs coming in, or coffee or rare Earth minerals going out. The small houses near the road have cement walls and red tile roofs. The poorer ones are made out of mud bricks. Occasionally, in the distance, the clouds and haze clear just enough to reveal the tops of the volcanoes to the north of us. It is breathtaking scenery no matter how many times I have seen it.

Then there is another clearing with rows of simple wooden poles about two meters tall covered with tarps. Men and women sit on rocks or stand, sorting coffee beans. Although I have seen this many times, my driver explains the coffee production process. I think he wants me to know how much work it is to bring that cup of coffee to my table. When we slow down around a curve, I can make out rows of jute sacks filled with the red-colored beans, and I see men arriving on bicycles with the sacks tied on them. And yes, I am forced to think of how many people and how much work it takes to get a single cup to our table.

From a distance, assuming you don't stop to ask questions and you don't read the human rights reports or my articles or books, and you don't know what has happened to Mary of Kivu and all the women like her, it looks like the place that Starbucks wants you to imagine that your coffee comes from.

There is nothing you see as you drive the winding roads around Lake Kivu that announces mass rape and continental war. Except perhaps the occasional white transport vehicle with the UN logo and the blue-helmeted men of various brown colors of skin. And the faces of women, which show a weariness that is heavier than in most other parts of Africa. The men mostly look down at the ground and rarely into your eyes. Except a few who are exactly the men you don't want looking into your eyes. Mary, I would come to find out, knew much about such men.

TWO

As I stepped into the hospital that day, seeking information about Mary of Kivu, I remembered the previous times I had been here. I remembered passing the wards where women smell of urine and children don't have the energy to swat flies off of their faces, and wards of bandaged men, some wounded by gunshots, others by *pangas*—machetes. On one of my previous visits, there were men outside the hospital gates saying they too had been raped. I had heard the hospital staff—the women staff—tell me that this was ludicrous. Later that same visit, I had heard a tall Congolese male nurse tell me, out of earshot of the female staff:

'I hear *mzungu* women say that here is the worst place on Earth to be a woman. I ask you: For men to do that kind of thing to women, what do you think is happening to *them*? To *us*, the men?'

His tone was not accusatory; rather it was filled with the same resignation I had seen on most of the faces here. I did not respond to his question. I don't think he had intended for me to.

Today, as I stepped into the office, I smiled and asked the nurse on duty what she knew about Mary of Kivu and if she had any idea where she lived. I have found that if I use French and Swahili and act as though I should be here, the hospital staff and officials of all kinds are usually happy to talk to *mzungus*, and to give me information they would probably not give out in hospitals and other official establishments in other parts of the world. I do not usually stop to ponder the ethics of this. Then again, after nearly two decades of conflict, giving out the name of a former patient is just as likely to be a humanitarian gesture as it is to be a breach of confidentiality.

I soon had the name of a village and of an international women's rights organization that had a local office near Mary's village and that might know how to find her.

I returned to my vehicle and my driver and I opened up a map of the Lake Kivu region. We found the town we guessed was the closest to the village where the woman said that Mary lived.

We were in the Land Cruiser for nearly three hours heading westward, away from the lake. We were on a mostly paved highway. The terrain and vegetation were much like that around the lake, with coffee and tea plantations, tracts of land with long-horned cattle grazing, banana tree farms, and the occasional village.

Finally, we turned off the main highway and entered Mary's territory. Soon we came to a village where I saw the signs I had seen on the Internet. In French and Swahili, they proclaimed that Mary was from here, that she had shopped here, and therefore, presumably, we would also want to.

We stopped at the market in the village and I saw the naïf paintings I had seen online, the ones in which she is posed like an African Virgin of Guadalupe.

She is painted as a tall, elegant African woman with a long skirt and matching head wrap. At her feet are villagers coming to be healed. She holds one hand up in a saint-like gesture.

There is a glowing disk around her head, which I take to be a halo, and around this portrait there is a straw wreath painted, serving to frame Mary's image in the painting.

I leaned down to hold up one of the paintings and a few minutes later I found that I had paid fifty dollars for one. My driver smiled at me as if I had done the typical *mzungu* thing, and then he carried the painting back to the car for me.

I continued walking through the market. The smells were familiar—fruit and meat on the edge of going bad and bodies that only had the luxury of bathing once every few days. A group of children, between the ages of four and eight, followed me, calling out *mzungu*. I turned and chased them for a moment, leaving them giggling uncontrollably. My driver watched this, at first with amusement and then with increasing impatience.

With a few questions to some women working in the market, we learned the location of the office of the international women's rights organization that had been mentioned to us, one of many organizations in the region that promote women's income generation and provide support to women who have been raped in the conflict.

The office was on a residential street, and was about twice the size of the houses near it. The name and logo of the organization were painted on the large metal gate. My driver stopped at the gate and honked and a nearly sleeping guard with eyes yellowed by malaria came out to our car. My driver explained that we were looking for Mary of Kivu and that we had been told that their organization could tell us how to find her. I held up my press card and my passport and the guard pretended to look at them and then he opened the gate to let our car pass.

He mumbled in French that I should go to the reception area at the end of the driveway.

There was an ample lawn around the building, which was essentially a larger version of the houses nearby: white stucco walls, red tile roofs, and large porches or overhangs. African women, and a few men, were coming and going from the reception area; others were climbing or descending the outside stairs that led to the second floor.

At the reception, an African woman with the eager look of a tour guide greeted me in French. I introduced myself, gave her my business card, and asked her if she might be able to help me find Mary of Kivu.

'You are not the only *mzungu* who wants to meet her,' the woman said, smiling.

As she said this, I noted a woman, a *mzungu*, with shoulder-length light brown hair walking down a nearby corridor.

'May I introduce you to her?' she asked, in the formal style that such things are often done here.

'Thanks, I'll introduce myself,' I said in French.

The *mzungu* woman was talking with another African woman. Behind them I could see a meeting room filled with at least a dozen African women, some with young children, all waiting in silence.

'Hi, I'm sorry to interrupt. I'm a journalist, Keith Masterson. I work and report in the region and I've been asked by my editor to do an interview with Mary of Kivu. Your colleague thought you might have an idea of where I could find her.'

I held out a business card. The woman, who was about my age, early thirties, and had pale, soft green eyes and was dressed in khaki, capri pants and a sleeveless African wax print blouse, turned and looked up at me, at first skeptical and then extended her hand. Her face softened. I could not easily place her in my *mzungu* categories. I would need more time for that.

'Hi, good to meet you. I'm Isabelle Pelleux. I work at our Europe regional office.'

There was an accent to her English. She turned and looked at the women behind her in the meeting room and then turned back to me as if she had forgotten something and just remembered it.

'You wrote that book on the Lord's Resistance Army, didn't you?' she asked.

'Yes I did.'

She nodded.

'I'm about to interview a group of women from around here about their experiences, and about what they know about Mary of Kivu. Maybe I can share with you some ideas when I'm done.'

'Great. I'd really appreciate it.'

I looked at the ground and then back up at her.

'Hey, um, I'm guessing you don't usually have men participate in these interviews, but do you think it would be okay if I sat in on it? I mean, we'd tell them who I am and why I'm here. Could be important to have their perspective in my story. I wouldn't use any names, of course.'

'I don't know,' she said. Her accent, which I guessed was French, was slightly stronger as she said this.

'How about this? We ask them if they'd be open to it and if they show any hesitation, I won't participate.'

She pondered this.

'Okay. But if they do agree to let you sit in, I ask the questions and I stop it if anything seems uncomfortable to them.'

'Yeah, absolutely. Thanks. I'll just get my bag and be right back. I want to get a notebook.'

When I came back from the jeep with my notebook, Isabelle was inside the meeting room with the women. The African woman she had been talking to in the hallway was acting as translator. I walked in.

'*Nina furaha sana kukutana na wewe,*' I said smiling, greeting the women in Swahili.

'*Karibu sana,*' they greeted me in return with big smiles.

The translator smiled as well. Isabelle looked on skeptically.

I asked the translator to explain who I was and to ask the women if it would be okay if I participated in the interview.

'It is okay. They say it is important for this to be known.'

* * *

There were twelve in total. Several had babies or young children with them, two of whom were sleeping, wrapped on tight with their cheeks pressed to their mothers' backs. The women were dressed in the Technicolor hues of the batik fabric I had seen in the market. Some had matching blouses and skirts; others wore T-shirts or faded polo shirts over their batik skirts. I watched as one of the small children squirmed in its mother's arms until the mother placed it on the floor. A moment later, the baby was peeing on the floor and began to cry. The mother did not notice the urine at first, and when she did she treated it as nothing more than water. She picked up the baby, and held her to her chest, oblivious to the urine dripping off of her baby's leg.

Another child, this one a toddler, kept staring at me with a frightened look; this was probably one of the few times he had seen *mzungus*. I smiled at him and gradually he stopped looking scared and teetered in my direction. Standing on wobbly legs, he leaned against my knee and then stopped there, looking up at me, gripping my knee and occasionally reaching out to my moving pen. I kept one eye on him and one on the group and would reach out my hand to steady him when he seemed about to fall.

As the women spoke, I had the feeling that I was hearing stories, stories especially tailored for *mzungus*, stories that were no less true but had been altered by each telling to *mzungus*.

There were stories of husbands who used violence, or who drank away their meager earnings from picking and processing coffee. Husbands who maintained second families. Stories of women who made money in microfinance projects and whose husbands went to spend even more money in bars. Several women nodded their heads at this. And there were stories of magic potions that could make wandering husbands return home. More women nodded their heads at this and uttered laughs and subtle vocalizations.

There were stories of rape, stories that nearly almost always started with: 'That day, when the soldiers came.' Then came the part that I can never understand: the husbands and families and villages that expel the women after they are raped. Isabelle asked why.

The list was long. The reasons were not judged by any of the women as being absurd or unfair; the motives were merely affirmed. It simply was so.

If we are allowed to stay in our villages, all the women in the village will miscarry.

They say a man got sick and almost died the night his wife came home after being a bush wife.

They say there will be drought.

There will be famine.

The children in the village will get sick and die or be born missing an arm or a leg.

The government road will not come through the village.

God will not shine his light upon us.

They say we are a shame to our families, that we brought it on ourselves, that we betrayed our husbands.

Our husbands cannot look at us anymore.

We cannot care for our husbands if they get sick. We cannot touch them.

They will make us pay back the bride price. Our husband's family will say that they paid for us for nothing.

Neither Isabelle nor I gave any reaction to these responses, although I thought I detected a combination of shock and rage in her eyes.

Isabelle was silent for a moment and in the lapse between her questions the women began laughing amongst themselves and saying many more words than the translator was translating. I could see in Isabelle's look that all of this was overwhelming for her—the children, the women, their stories.

And then they seemed to notice Isabelle, noticed her beyond the whiteness of her skin, beyond her role as some-one important in her organization—noticed her as a woman. The translator looked shy as she translated their questions. At first she started each sentence saying: '*They* want to know.' And then she simply said to Isabelle: 'Did you …?' or 'Are you …?'

Do you have children?

Isabelle shook her head.

'No, not yet. I'm not sure if I want to have children.'

Do you have a husband? Doesn't he want children from you?

Isabelle shook her head again.

No husband? Why not?

'I was almost married,' Isabelle said. 'I mean, yes, we were like married, living together.'

Isabelle stopped and let the translator catch up. The women were perplexed.

'But it didn't work out,' Isabelle continued.

The women stared at Isabelle as if they needed some kind of explanation. In this part of the world, for a marriage not to work out there must be something horrible, something Isabelle did, or perhaps she was barren, or worse. I couldn't tell if Isabelle knew this; it seemed that she did not.

Was he violent toward you? they asked.

Again, Isabelle was silent. They were staring at her, waiting.

'No. It's just that he was interested in different things than I was. He didn't respect my work, and that I have to travel for work. And he cannot take care of me. He can barely take care of himself. I can't imagine him caring for a child, let alone for me if I were to get sick or really need him to take care of me— all the things I want in a partner.'

She said this rapid-fire in French; I could see a slight desperation in the translator's eyes.

Did his family pay many cows or goats for you?

'We don't really do that where I come from. Sometimes he may give you a gold ring.'

Did you go back to your father's house when you left him?

'No, I didn't. I live by myself.'

Isabelle paused for a moment. She was slowly getting better at responding when they needed an explanation.

'That's what we do where I am from.'

At this they all nodded and one of them spoke.

God makes all men the same.

They laughed and Isabelle laughed back. And then they looked at me.

'What do you think of that, Mr. Masterson?' Isabelle said.

The women laughed as this was translated.

I shrugged.

'I'm not married either,' I said. 'I travel far too much. But when I do get married, I think I'll know how to take care of my wife and respect her. I hope I will. That's what my mother taught me to do. And since I am a good son, I *always* listen to her.'

I smiled and they laughed. They did not need to know more about me; they did not need to know the real me. We were all giving performances.

The small boy leaning against my knee looked up at the women laughing and he too smiled. When there was silence again, Isabelle continued.

'What do you know about Mary?'

Several of the women began talking at the same time. It was approaching dusk when they finished. I scribbled furiously the entire time.

She told me to go to my house right away because I would find my husband having sex with my young sister. She told me get my children and leave him. She was right.

She touched my mother's head. My mother had been sick in the head for years, and after Mary touched her she was well.

She cured that child. Right in front of me.

They all nodded at these accounts. Some said: 'Hallelujah'

Then one said: 'And she kept the baby. And she loves it. That is unbelievable. Incredible. Only a saint could do that. After what happened.'

They all became silent after that. I wished I could have asked questions but I wanted to honor my deal with Isabelle. I wished that she had asked more about Mary's baby and what had happened. I was sure it was going to disappoint me, that it was going to be something based on superstition, something that would seem silly in Western eyes. Still, I wanted to hear what they said.

* * *

As the interview ended, I led the small boy who had been leaning on my knee back to his mother and I nodded at the women, and shook the hands of those who came up to me. Isabelle was already outside with the translator and some other African women from the NGO.

'Thanks, really, for letting me sit in on this. I hope that wasn't too awkward,' I said to Isabelle, as I stepped out of the room.

'Not for them. Maybe for me,' she said, with a somewhat forced smile.

'Hey, another question before I take off,' I said. 'Does your organization have a guesthouse around here that they recommend?'

'Yeah, there's a simple one, but it's decent. Have your driver talk to Sophie in the reception. She can give you directions. It's the same one I'm staying in.'

* * *

The guesthouse was simple but clean, with a small garden out back with white plastic tables and chairs. The rooms were off of two corridors, as orderly as a convent; the only decorative touch was the African wax print cloth used for the curtains and bedspreads. Plus the electricity was on when I checked in, which was a good sign.

As I signed the guest register, I told the woman at the front desk that I would be staying three nights at the most. I was sure I would be gone by then—interview in hand, hoax revealed. The story, even if interesting, would take no more than a day or two to gather, and I would return, with relief, to the Rwandan side of the border. I had no idea that I would be here much longer than I expected, and that I would come to know the guesthouse staff by name, and meet their children. And that they would come to know things about me.

THREE

The next morning I saw Isabelle at breakfast and sat down at the same table. Her hair was pulled up and she was wearing a longish, Indian-style blouse over jeans.

'How did you get involved in this work?' she asked. 'I mean, become interested in this region and the conflicts?'

I smiled; this was a standard opening for conversations among *mzungus* in the heart of darkness. I usually preferred this conversation over a bottle of beer at the end of a day, not at the beginning of one, or I avoided it altogether.

'I'd have to blame my father,' I said. 'He's a photojournalist, chased wars and conflicts, all the ones of the 1980s and 1990s. You've probably seen his work. He won the Pulitzer for a series of photos he took in the Balkans. There is a famous one he took of a young woman who was kept as a sex slave.'

I paused, letting her acknowledge if she knew the photo I was talking about; I had had this conversation before with other *mzungus*.

'No, I mean, well, maybe I have seen it, but I don't recall,' she said.

'Anyway,' I said, continuing, 'I did a master's in anthropology, studying conflict and religion in Africa, how traditional rituals and religious beliefs are manipulated in conflicts. Studied French and Swahili. Spent some time here, and in Rwanda and in Burundi. An article I wrote led to a contract for a book on the Lord's Resistance Army. I spent about a year in Uganda and in the Sudan researching that book. Now I'm writing a book on rituals and the roots of the Congolese conflict.'

'Will you show me your father's pictures sometime?' she asked.

'Sure. I've got some on my laptop. And you? How did you end of up here?'

'I can blame my parents as well. My mother was a political refugee from Chile during the Pinochet years. I grew up hearing stories of what they did to women, to the political prisoners, that is.'

Her voice lapsed into a slightly Spanish-inflected accent as she said this, or maybe it was just my imagination. But I am almost sure her 'i's sounded like Spanish 'i's.

'And then we lived in Asia and I saw, you know, the ways girls and women are treated. I did a master's in gender studies focusing on women in Africa and Asia. Then I got a job with our NGO. I wanted to make a difference.'

She paused; she must have seen the cynicism in my eyes or she had read it in my book.

'I think we can do some good here,' she continued. 'I hope that we can. But at the same time there is so much bullshit. The fundraising, those stories we have to write to individual donors so they feel they are saving a particular woman. The celebrities who come for ten minutes and then leave. Some of it makes sense and we have to do it, but sometimes, well, you know what I'm talking about. There is only so much we can do for the women.'

I think she could see in my eyes that I was relieved to know she wasn't a doe-eyed optimist.

'And then so much we cannot do,' she continued.

She said she had meetings at her office but that she could meet me in the afternoon to go together to Mary's house. I thought my chances of getting an interview with Mary of Kivu were better if I was with a woman, particularly one from a women's rights organization. We fixed a time to meet.

* * *

I started my day with an interview with the priest at the Catholic church in the village. I had asked my driver to gather some information and identify potential sources, and he suggested we start here.

'They say he knows Mary and that he knows what you have to do to get an interview with her,' my driver said.

It was a fairly simple church by Catholic standards—basic cinderblock walls with whitewash around the base of the few trees and a simple, white plaster virgin out front.

The receptionist led me down a hallway to the priest's office. The floor was polished linoleum tile and there were gaps covered with screens in the cinderblocks that served as windows. There were several portraits of Mary of Nazarene and wooden crosses on the walls.

The priest's office was equally simple, with a large window framed by embroidered curtains and a dark wooden desk. Behind the desk were gray metal bookshelves filled with books, most in English.

The priest rose to shake my hand. He was an elegant-looking African man, just the slightest grey around his temples; by his accent I guessed he must have been Anglophone East African.

'Hello, Father ... ' I began, realizing my driver had not given me his name.

'Father Ningonwe,' he said. 'You must be the *mzungu* journalist they mentioned.'

'Keith Masterson. A pleasure to meet you. I ... '

'Yes, I recognize your name. I have seen some of your articles. You have a famous book, I think.'

'I guess you know that I'm trying to interview Mary of Kivu.'

'Yes, yes, I know. Everyone wants to find out more about Mary of Kivu,' he said.

'I was hoping ... '

'You know,' he continued, interrupting me, 'if she were European, they would already have sent someone from the Vatican to conduct an investigation as to whether these were truly miracles. And what action the Church should take. But we get far fewer of such visits here than in Latin America or say, the Philippines. I have sent my request, but they say they are still deciding.'

He paused to look at me and then continued.

'We don't have many African saints. If it were to come to that. And most of the ones we do have are North African. If you stretch it, you can probably count a dozen or two at the most. That's not many in the history of the Roman Catholic Church. Then again, not surprising.'

I wasn't sure where this was headed but I decided to wait before I asked him directly if he could help me get to Mary.

'How long have you been in this parish?' I asked.

'Since the first round of the conflict. Right after the genocide and when the conflict came this direction. I thought I would work in Rwanda. I thought I would have a parish there. But they told me I was needed in Congo. This is where they need us now.'

He looked at me again.

'Which you know much about.'

I nodded. I had written the paragraphs countless times of how eastern Congo became inflamed after the Rwandan genocide in 1994. About the leaders of the Rwandan genocide, Hutus, who headed into eastern Congo, now the Democratic Republic of Congo, when the Tutsis and moderate Hutus, under the Rwandan Patriotic Front, took over the country. Tens of thousands of Hutus fled, as refugees, worried they would face reprisals from the Tutsis. Some of the Hutus stayed armed inside Congo, threatening to return to Rwanda. The Rwandan government, which as my previous Congolese driver had said, knows how to run an army, entered Congo to pursue the *genocidaires*. This incursion inspired nearly every other country in the region to send troops into some portion of Congo, all with their own motives, in the period known here, but nearly unknown to most of the rest of the world, as the Great African War. Numerous bands of armed groups, including the Mai Mai, sprang up to defend their communities in the face of the inept Congolese military (and sometimes to defend their villages *from* the Congolese military). And although Rwandan troops withdrew long ago, the Rwandan government has sporadically supported some of the militias in an effort to defend Congolese Tutsis or to attack the ex-*genocidaires*, or both. These armed groups continue to operate, fueled in no small part by the vast mineral wealth in the region. They sometimes pillage villages and rape women.

I kept that summary paragraph on my computer, ready to

insert as necessary in an article. Most *mzungus* looked hopelessly lost when I tried to explain. In terms of lives lost, it is the deadliest war in the world in the past twenty years, yet few *mzungus* know even the most basic facts about it.

'She won't see you, you know,' he finally said.

'No?'

'She doesn't talk about herself and about what she does.'

I nodded again.

'Do you think it's true?' I asked.

'The miracles? I don't know that it matters what I believe. The people here believe. And we shall see what the Vatican says.'

He leaned back and interlaced his fingers as if he were about to retreat into silence and reflection, or give me priestly advice after a confession.

'How do you get to see her if you want her help?' I asked.

'Honestly, I don't know what it takes to get Mary to receive you and talk to you. I know that it's mostly women that she receives. Although I've heard of a few men being received too. I've not heard of her receiving a *mzungu*, though. And I know that she turns away requests for interviews.'

'So how does she decide which ones she'll see?'

'Are you in need of a miracle, Mr. Masterson? Of healing? Forgiveness, maybe?'

I smiled and shrugged. 'Not that I know of,' I said.

'Well, then,' he said and pushed his chair back slowly and stood up. 'Good luck.'

'Thank you,' I said. 'I wish you luck as well. Certainly this region deserves its share of saints.'

'Yes, I suppose we do,' he said. 'Although I'm not sure they've done you that much good in the West.'

* * *

I met Isabelle back at her organization at the agreed hour. She was sitting outside on one of the chairs under an overhang, talking with two African women. They were looking at some documents together and nodding their heads. She excused herself and walked toward me.

'Find out anything?' she asked.

'Not really. Except that she doesn't give interviews.'

'Well, let's try,' she said, her voice energetic.

'Shall we take my car?' I asked.

'Sure. I assume you won't mind waiting if she agrees to see me,' she said.

'No, not at all,' I said opening the door to the jeep for her. 'And I hope you won't mind waiting for me if she agrees to see me.'

'I somehow doubt she'll see a man, from what I've heard, and a journalist at that.'

'You never know,' I said, smiling.

She did not return the smile, but I noticed that her face was soft even when serious; there was a girlish quality about it. She had high cheekbones and a noble nose, and she had a slightly lopsided smile that was perhaps the only asymmetrical part of her face.

'I heard she asks women, well, mostly women, to bring a letter or to write her a letter explaining their need,' Isabelle said.

'Do you have one?' I asked.

'No, but I could probably make up something if I had to.'

Again, she was serious.

'How often do you come to the region?' I asked.

37

'This is my first time. I've been to East Africa but never here before. You've been to Congo and the Lake Kivu region many times, I guess.'

'Yeah, I'm living here on and off at the moment.'

'How do you keep a life back home?'

'You're assuming that I have a life back home.'

'I see.'

'And you? I didn't ask you where home is.'

'Geneva.'

'Are you from there?'

'Yes, more or less. My father is Swiss, my mother is Chilean, I think I told you. My father is a diplomat. We were posted in Latin America several times and once in Asia, and then we moved to Geneva when my sisters and I were older.'

She glanced at me; I felt I was being assessed.

'You must be pleased with your book on the Lord's Resistance Army. It did well, no? I saw several reviews. Mostly good ones. Even the negative ones criticize you for things I thought were important to include. You know, the bullshit side of our international aid work.'

'Yeah, it, um, lets me make a living doing this.'

Now she looked away from me and down to the ground; it was as if she hid her eyes from time to time, as if they needed to be shielded from the light occasionally, or from direct gazes. Perhaps it meant that I was staring too intently.

'I don't think she'll see you,' she said. 'I'm fine to have you come along but I think that since she knows our organization, and knows about our work with women, the economic empowerment, the health services and all, that she will likely see me.'

'Yeah, of course. If I don't get to see her, I'll interview some other people and you can share with me what you feel comfortable sharing.'

'Yes. Okay.'

A few minutes later, we passed through a hilly area of coffee plantations and then came into a large expanse of tea cultivation, with rows of vivid green tea bushes. I saw a sign with the name of the tea company.

As we passed them, I remembered why I find tea plantations relaxing. They are orderly, with the smallest of trails between rows of bushes, trails that seem to invite you to take a solitary walk. Workers usually pick in small numbers so the fields never seem crowded. And from a distance, with their tiny variations, the leaves look as if they would be soft to the touch.

'That's where Joseph works, her husband. I am told he's the manager of that tea estate,' my driver said.

After we passed the tea estate, there was another village, one with well-constructed houses, painted cinder blocks with recently constructed zinc roofs; most were one-story and looked to have two or three bedrooms inside. There was a small Catholic church and a market with fruits and vegetables on display. Then as we rounded a curve in the road, I knew we had arrived.

There were several hundred people in front of the house. On one side of the road, there was a line, mostly of women dressed in the usual bright color African waxprint wrappers. The smaller number of men were dressed as if going to church, in baggy dress shirts and slacks that sat high on their waists. Some wore mismatched blazers. Some of the women were standing, but most were sitting on the ground. There were some women reclining, and at least a few elderly women and men were on makeshift stretchers; I guessed they had been carried there. A few younger men were carrying plastic containers with drinks and women and children were selling different kinds of food.

Just outside the compound of the house there was an area cordoned off with a tent-like roof sheltering some simple tables.

My driver looked back to Isabelle and me and pointed.

'That is where people present their letters and stories and needs. They'll tell you what to do,' he said.

Isabelle and I looked at each other and stepped out of the jeep. We walked over to the tent. There was a serious-looking woman sitting on a white plastic chair behind a folding table that sat toward the back of the tent. She was apparently reading letters. She seemed to be a gatekeeper.

'Hello. I'm Isabelle Pelleux, with the organization that … '

'Hmm,' the woman said with the dismissive air of a government bureaucrat, giving only a quick glance up at us.

'I'm Keith Masterson. I'm a journalist. I've written several books about the conflict here and, well, we're very interested in Mary's story and would be very pleased … '

'She won't see you,' the woman said firmly in French, finally looking up at us.

'Is it possible to show her our business cards and at least ask her? We can wait,' I said.

'With all of them waiting?' the woman said, pointing to the line.

'We're not here for the same reason,' Isabelle said, using just the slightest condescending tone.

'Of course,' I said in a more conciliatory tone. 'We understand how busy Mary is. How busy you all are with your important work. If you could just ask her. We can come back later. Or if she just has time to talk to one of us, then Ms. Pelleux can go with her.'

The woman was silent for a moment; I think she hoped we would leave.

'Eh, between sessions I will tell her,' the woman said finally, in the same dismissive voice, and then held out her hand for our business cards.

'But I tell you again, she will not see either of you. And a journalist, I know she won't. You are wasting your time.'

The woman left the tent and walked in the direction of the main house and we waited. There were more letters delivered to another woman who came to occupy the table, and then names were called and more women went inside. I heard cases pleaded in Swahili and in French. I took notes on two of them. I looked at my mobile phone many times; on and off it had a signal. I felt eyes on me, and on us.

I could tell that Isabelle did not want to talk. And I was back at work, noting details and thinking about how to get interesting interviews with the women in line.

Finally, after nearly an hour, the woman who first received us came back to the tent.

'You two come,' she said to us.

We were both surprised and quickly followed her. She led us to one side of the house, where there was a small porch area with about six chairs. It felt like the backstage of a performance space, the kind of place I'd waited to interview Mai Mai warlords. It always amazed me how, in the middle of the bush, they could set up a human perimeter around themselves— projecting an aura of the big, big man, even if all they lorded over was a handful of malnourished, stoned young men with secondhand guns.

Mary came out. She looked young; I would have guessed early twenties. But her face had a weight or somberness that suggested she was older than that. She had an elegant, almost sculptural nose and forehead, both dramatized by her head-wrap. Her impeccable African wax print dress was in blues and greens and looked as if it had just been ironed. She was as tall and striking as the naïf paintings portrayed her. There were two women trailing her like chiefs of staff, both holding folders that evidently contained letters and lists of names.

Isabelle and I both instinctively stood up. I worked to keep myself from jumping up and pleading my case.

I saw one of the assistants look at Isabelle and I heard her say, between words in Swahili, the name of the NGO. Mary nodded in understanding and she looked at Isabelle, who gave her the slightest smile. The assistant did not show Mary my card. I was already looking off in the distance, readying myself for the inevitable no.

And then I heard Mary say the word *mtu*, man in Swahili.

Mary and her assistants walked back into the house.

A few minutes later, the dismissive woman from the front entrance came back out.

'She will see Mr. Keith. Tomorrow. Come early in the morning.'

I looked up, startled, and saw how surprised Isabelle looked.

'Why not *me*?' Isabelle said in rapid-fire French.

'She says Mr. Keith needs her help.'

This time I started to wrinkle my eyebrows but made myself nod.

'I'll be back tomorrow morning. *Asante sana*,' I said.

Without saying anything else, Isabelle and I walked out through the yard, past the line, and to the jeep.

'I have no idea what that means,' I said to Isabelle, as we got back in the jeep.

'Me neither,' she said, giving a slightly strained smile. 'I hope you'll tell me what you learn.'

'Absolutely.'

'What do you think she meant by saying that you need Mary's help?'

'I have no idea.'

We were both silent during the nearly hour drive back to the guesthouse.

FOUR

I was not sure if Isabelle was displeased by what had happened, or if she simply did not want to talk on our return journey from Mary's house to our guesthouse. In the silence, as the sun set and the inside of the jeep became dark, I thought about the last time I had been around someone like Mary, someone who could supposedly heal and see things that the rest of us could not. That made me think about Sienna and the way things had ended.

Sienna and I were both studying for master's degrees in anthropology at the University of North Carolina. We met during our first semester. At the end of our first year, we were in Brazil doing field work together. As part of the trip, a group of fellow graduate students went to an *Umbanda* ceremony, a ritual of one of the African-Brazilian religions, in Fortaleza, in the northeast of Brazil. An American colleague of one of our professors was friends with the *pai-de-santo*, the leader of the ceremony—the one who channels the spirits.

The *pai-de-santo* was drinking *cachaça* when we arrived and was smoking a strong-smelling cigar. He welcomed us with the few words of English he knew. As we greeted him, his helpers—the drummers—arrived and sat next to him. It was a hot night and the house was small and the windows were closed.

Soon the worshippers settled into their places, men on one side and women on the other, all of us standing. There were at least thirty-five of us in total. I moved to the men's side and leaned with my back against the wall. I started to cross my arms but was told that this was not allowed. We were to leave them open to receive the spirits that might come into us.

The lights were dimmed and the drumming started, the heavy cigar smoke lingering in the hot air. For a few minutes there was no sound but the drumming, and it felt to me as if there was not enough air for all of us in this small room.

Then the *pai-de-santo* began spinning, his eyes tightly closed, and started muttering words that made no sense to me either in Portuguese or English. His voice sounded as if he had inhaled helium, and was nothing like his pre-trance voice.

Continuing to spin, he raised a hand and twirled a few times more, until his palm came crashing down on the forehead of one of the worshippers. A few seconds later this worshipper began spinning and muttering unintelligible words. The other worshippers held out their arms so the person did not crash into a wall.

This continued a few times and I found myself aligning my head so it was exactly behind the head of a person standing in front of me, trying to reduce the chance that the *pai-de-santo* would find me. I was not sure what I would do if his hand came crashing down on my forehead.

On one particular go around, the *pai-de-santo* held his hand near the forehead of the man in front of me. And then, although I could swear his eyes were closed, the *pai-de-santo* passed his hand around the head of the man in front of me and brought it crashing down exactly in the middle of my forehead.

As I felt the pain on the back of my head from being pushed against the brick wall, I looked up and saw Sienna watching me from the woman's side of the room. Her eyes were wide open, as if she were worried that I might start spinning and speaking in tongues. I saw concern in her eyes and then I saw her smile. It was a warm and engulfing smile, and it was absolutely transparent in expressing what she felt for me.

I broke up with her the week after we got back to university.

* * *

'Why, Keith?' Sienna had asked me.

'I can't really tell you. I just know it's not going to … '

'What is it? I'm not right? We're not right? The moment's not right? What is it?'

Her voice went from sadness to warmth to accusation.

'I don't know.'

'You don't know or you don't want to tell me because you think you'll hurt me more?'

'I don't know.'

'Keith, I'd rather know the truth and be hurt than not know and hurt for even longer.'

'It's just not working.'

'Right.'

'I just don't want this now. It's too much … '

'Right.'

'I have to go. I'm sorry. Really, I am.'

'Right.'

But it was not over.

* * *

When Isabelle and I arrived at the guesthouse, I made an excuse to be on my own.

'Hey, uh, I'm going to go into town to use Internet. It's really slow in the guesthouse and I need to respond to a few e-mails, send some documents,' I said.

I didn't invite her to accompany me. Although I was intrigued by the conversation of the morning, I was not, for the moment, in the mood for more.

'Okay, I'm going to stay here. I'm exhausted,' she said.

When I arrived at the Internet café, I got a password from the clerk and plugged the modem cable into my laptop. The café was painted a dark blue inside, which gave it the feel of a jazz club, and as darkness fell it seemed that the only light was that coming from the computers.

First I sent a message to Sam that I had apparently managed to get an interview with Mary.

'Keep expectations low,' I wrote, 'but I'm trying.'

Seconds later, he shot back: 'Ian says send him what you have as soon as you can. *The New Yorker* is interested.'

Then I saw a message from my mother. The title said: 'News about your father.'

I don't know what I expected. They had so little contact with each other—none really. Usually I was the one who informed the other about something major in their lives. I couldn't imagine what my father would be in touch with my mother about.

My Dearest Keith –
I can't recall this week which country you're in. I tried your mobile and it says you're out of area. This is not news I wanted to give you by e-mail but I thought you should know.

I heard via your uncle Randall that your father was diagnosed yesterday with esophageal cancer. They don't know yet if it's metastasized but they think it's Stage III, which means it's all the way through the esophageal tissue and in the surrounding lymph nodes. The doctors are still studying the best course of action—chemo or radiation or both, or even surgery. He's probably had the symptoms for some time but took it to be a cough or gastric reflux. And, just like Lyndon, he waited far too long to get it looked at. Randall says your father finally stopped smoking but I guess not soon enough. I'm so sorry to hear about this, sorry for you. Call me when you can. I hope you're well and I hope you can reach your father. If I can help in any way, let me know. Will sends his love.
With all my love—Mom

Here was the *pai-de-santo* again. Here was the hand reaching around the person I was hiding behind and finding my head and smashing it against the wall.

FIVE

At breakfast the next morning, Isabelle could tell from my silence and the tense look on my face that something was bothering me. When she asked what it was, I told her about my father.

'I'm so sorry,' she said, and then she was quiet for a moment. 'Will you go see him?'

I looked out the window of the guesthouse to the road that passed nearby.

'He hasn't been much of a father. He and my mother divorced years ago. After his Pulitzer he became an asshole. Or maybe he already was and that's just when I realized it.'

She asked for another cup of coffee and gave me a look that told me she wanted to know more and that she had time to listen.

'I think the first time I started to figure him out, I was maybe in third grade. That was when he and my mom split up. He came home during the day, which wasn't normal for him. He was in his usual work uniform of khaki pants, a light blue Oxford shirt that hadn't been ironed, and his old brown leather jacket. I saw that he had a cut on his face and a bruise around his eye that he kept touching. I asked him what happened.

'He told me it was nothing, just a brief altercation.

'Then I saw my mother standing in the doorway to the living room. She worked at a nearby art gallery then, and was home most afternoons when I was younger. She just stood there in the doorway with her arms crossed.'

As I described this to Isabelle, I could see that version of my mother, circa 1985: she had long brown hair, shampoo-commercial-shiny-straight cut, wearing jeans and a black sweater.

'It took me a little while but then I understood. My father had been taking a picture when it happened. The person who got mad at him had pushed the camera into his face and left a bruise and mark in the shape of the viewfinder.

'So my mother asked him what he had been taking pictures of. I couldn't understand why she was so mad at him. Then, a few weeks later, I heard doors slamming. I was in my room and I hear my mom yelling at him.

"Where are the pictures?!" she yelled at him. And he told her to calm down, that there's no picture, that there's no one else.

'I didn't know what she meant, right? So he told her: "Louise, please calm down. There's no picture. There's no one … " And she yelled that he was lying and then my dad was yelling: "Louise, please don't open those."

'Then there were more doors slamming. My father was not there for breakfast the next morning. When I asked where he was, my mother said that he had to travel again for work. He never came back.'

I paused and felt Isabelle looking at me.

'Are you in touch with him? I mean has he been involved in your life?' she asked.

'Not much, really. My mother found a job in Arizona, at a gallery there, and so we moved and after that I saw him much less. I would see him in New York once a year.'

'And your mother?'

'She was angry for a long time, like two years. She would try not to show it to me, or take it out on me. She'd apologize and say it wasn't my fault and then when she started to talk about how horrible my father was, she'd stop and get this look.'

Isabelle looked intently at me.

'She'd smile, or force herself to smile. "This isn't for us to talk about, honey. He's your father. It's between him and me." Then she'd be quiet for hours or days. It was just the two of us in the house for those couple of years and she could go for a day saying just a few words to me.'

Isabelle nodded.

'And now, how is she? How is she taking this?'

'She's beyond it. She met Will, my stepfather, two or three years after we moved to Arizona. He's really a nice guy, and he's good to her. And since then she got her smile back and I got my mother back.'

I looked out the window.

'When he became famous because of that photo in the Balkans, I started to find out more about him. Women he was with in different countries. My mom was looking for pictures of all those women. She was taking the film out of his cameras.'

Isabelle continued to look at me, shaking her head.

'Sorry, that's more than you needed to know.'

'That's fine,' she said.

'I always swore I'd be nothing like him.'

* * *

My driver and I made the now familiar drive. The line outside Mary's house was as long as it had been the day before. I went to the table again but this time a different woman was doing the gatekeeping.

'Hi, I'm Keith Masterson. I'm a journalist. I was here yesterday and the woman who was here arranged for Mary to see me today, for an interview.'

The woman looked up at me briefly.

'You have to tell your story. We read them and Mary chooses who she sees. It helps if you have extra support. Letters from the priest or a pastor about your problem.'

'I'm a journalist. I don't have a story to tell her. I came to interview her. I want to know *her* story.'

'That's not how it works. You have to tell her *your* story.'

'My story?'

'Yes. Your problem. What you need her help with. If she has accepted you it is because you need help. She *must* know what it is.'

I worked to control my frustration.

'Can you just go talk to the other staff who were here yesterday? They will tell you that Mary herself said she would see me.'

The woman looked at me again; I recognized the bureaucratic style. Without a word she left another woman in charge and walked to Mary's house.

A few minutes later, the first woman who received me came back to the tent.

'Mary will see you on Tuesday.'

'Tuesday? That's four days from now. That's a long time to wait to see her. I … '

The woman glared at me and then looked toward the women, men and children in the long line. She seemed to focus her eyes on an area where there were four or five people on stretchers.

'Would you say your needs are greater than these here waiting?' she said.

That question again. I breathed deeply. Rarely did warlords or gun smugglers leave me waiting so long.

'No, of course not,' I said. 'I will come back next Tuesday.'

'Ask for Mary's sister. She will introduce you to Mary.'

As I began to leave, I heard the sound of ululating voices and women singing, coming from the direction of the house. The women were dressed in matching reds, oranges, and yellows, all wearing headwraps of the same color. I leaned back toward my driver, looking at him expectantly.

'Let's go,' he said. 'We can do nothing but wait.'

As we walked away, the women continued to sing and shout.

'What happened? What are they singing?' I asked my driver.

'They are singing that our sister Mary has healed another.'

* * *

I had other stories I was working on; I had notes to write up and edit and send to Sam. A few weeks earlier I had managed to get an interview with one of the most notorious Mai Mai warlords in South Kivu, one responsible for some of the worst atrocities in the region—atrocities I had trouble even describing in the article.

I heard from the man's teachers and parents that he had been a model student going into secondary school—calm, obedient.

Then the girl he liked and swore he would marry began going out with a young soldier, a new recruit in the Congolese armed forces, which had established a presence in town, supposedly to keep it safe from invading Rwandan troops. The once calm boy became possessed, his parents said. He ran away for hours at a time and began drinking and getting into fights at school over the smallest provocation. In his wanderings in the bush, he came across a cell of Mai Mai fighters and they took him in.

He wouldn't tell me about their rituals, about what they did to him in the bush, or what he did in the bush. I learned about his atrocities from others in the village. He devised the cruelest of plans against Congolese soldiers, particularly ones they found by themselves, and against the households that were known to feed or offer a room for the soldiers. It was estimated that one out of every three women and girls in the village were raped in a two-week rampage that he led.

At the time I interviewed him, he was part of the official Congolese armed forces. One of the ways the Congolese government tried to end the worst atrocities by groups like the Mai Mai was to invite their combatants to become part of the official army. We met once at his barracks and a second time in his house outside the base. He had married another woman, a girl really, not more than seventeen, one that he had first taken by force as a bush wife when he was still with the Mai Mai. But he swore that he was still in love with the girl from his school.

Instead of an interview, it seemed he wanted my advice about his love life. Being *mzungu*, he thought I knew all things about how to win over women. He told me that he would leave his current wife in an instant if his first love would have him. She was now married to a military officer.

'Do you think she'll have me now?' he said. 'Now that I have a uniform just like him?'

He cleaned his fingernails with a knife as he asked this; I could see that two of his fingernails were missing.

He had commanded his men to rape schoolgirls, dragging them out in the middle of class and making the rest of the village watch. I had trouble even writing down what he and his men had done to the women and girls and to the soldiers they caught. He had taken a girl from the town to be his sex slave in the bush. And now he wondered if his childhood sweetheart would have him back.

The interview was part of one of my chapters on the motivations of the Mai Mai and other armed groups. As I looked at my notes again, I thought: Maybe Mary was right. Maybe I did need help. My father was likely dying of cancer, and I had these stories in my head. Sienna was very far away, and there were things we still had to resolve. Of course I needed help.

SIX

While I waited the days until my first interview with Mary, I decided to spend the weekend writing at a lakeside lodge on Lake Kivu, almost three hours by car from Mary's village. Before I left, I looked for Isabelle to see if she would still be here when I returned, but I did not see her. I told the woman at the guesthouse to tell Isabelle that I would be back on Sunday.

The lodge on the lake was filled with young couples (mostly *mzungus* but a few African) and missionaries. There were simple rows of white lodges with views of the lake surrounded by the dramatic green hills and mountains. Some of the buildings were one story, others two. I sat in the balcony of my first floor, lakefront room or in the restaurant and wrote, looking up occasionally at the view or at the bats or birds that swooped in my direction.

The hotel restaurant was lakeside; at one end of it there was a ladder for climbing into or out of the lake. Beyond that was a small dock area from where boat tours departed. I watched African couples dressed in their finest Sunday clothes board the boats, the men helping the women in high heels step on and off.

I played my familiar role of being invisible. With a notebook, a laptop, or a book in front of me, I could go for hours without being interrupted or spoken to, except perhaps by waitstaff. This is how I like to work, especially in this part of

Africa, where being a *mzungu* means that I always stand out.

I talked to my mother briefly via telephone and she told me how sorry she was about my father. She worked so hard not to be bitter about him—not to let her disappointment affect my relationship with him.

'I suggested that Randall write you directly with updates.'

I could tell that she wanted to ask me if I would call my father.

Sunday morning, before I returned to Mary's village, I went for a long run through a village near the lodge. I ran over rocky roads of red dirt and saw huts and mud-brick houses, and goats and cattle. I saw tall boys with long walking sticks in their hands guarding cattle; some of them stood so still that they seemed to be sleeping standing up. One of them looked up at me lazily and smiled, showing a huge gap between his teeth.

I saw women and children emerging from their round huts. Some waved at me as I ran by. For a few minutes, two boys about six or seven years old, both in shorts and shirts too big for them, ran alongside me, laughing, trying to keep up. They were barefoot.

Then three girls joined us. They ran in sandals. I turned to look at them. Two of the girls were older, probably eight or nine. One was much younger, maybe four or five years old, and we all slowed down slightly so she could keep up.

I looked at the littlest girl for a moment, this tiny African girl wearing a faded jeans skirt and a multi-colored, African print top. Her cheeks were slightly rounded and healthy and she had a bright look in her eyes. I saw that she was reaching her hand out. I thought she was reaching it out to me and I slowed a bit more to take hold of it. She looked up when I took her hand and she quickly pulled away, reaching instead for one of the girls next to her.

* * *

I returned to the guesthouse at the end of the day on Sunday and on Monday morning was back in Mary's village. I spent Monday doing interviews—trying to find backstory. I had not seen Isabelle either the night before or Monday morning before I left for the interviews. The staff at the guesthouse told me she was still staying there. I wanted to see her again.

I asked my driver to take me to the school where we had seen the sign that said 'Mary studied here.'

It was, like the Catholic church where I had met Father Ningonwe, also of simple, cinder-block construction. It was clean and well-kept (not adjectives I would use for all of the other places we visited) and had the feel of a traditional, girls' boarding school. There were four buildings on the compound, a combination of classrooms and dormitories. After asking around I found out that the current headmistress had been one of Mary's teachers.

A nun led me down the hallway of the school administration building. She was short and probably in her sixties. She shuffled her feet slightly as we walked down the halls, which had plain white walls and cement floors. It was nearing exam period, she told me, so the girls were in the their rooms studying. She liked the quiet, she said.

The headmistress was probably in her sixties as well, maybe her seventies, although except for a slight neck tremor, it would

58

have been impossible to tell if she were forty-five or sixty-five. She had no gray in her hair; the only thing that gave away her age was the tremor and the texture of the skin around her eyes.

I didn't even have to ask a question. Simply announcing the topic of Mary of Kivu got her going.

'She was an excellent student,' the headmistress said, her head slightly shaking and her voice slightly wavering with all the poise of an African Katherine Hepburn. 'Smart. Excellent in English and French. Wanted to be a teacher. Taught here for a time. As an assistant teacher.'

She stopped for a moment as if gathering her thoughts.

'Oh, but her mind became unfocused when she met Joseph. Happens to too many of our girls. He wanted her to finish her studies. She did, but it wasn't easy for her. He had gone away to study, in Uganda. And I seem to recall there was some trouble with Joseph's brother, too. What was his name?'

She was silent for a moment, and then looked at me as if she thought I might know. Out the window where she seemed to be looking, I could see the bright red flowers of an Umuko tree.

'She was a pretty one. Still is. There's always more than one after the pretty ones, isn't there? Well, I guess you would know about that. You've probably chased your share. Now, her wedding, that was a thing to see. We're a simple village, but well off compared to some around here. That was an affair.'

She stopped as if she did not have anything else to add.

'And what about the miracles and all that's happening now? What do you make of all this?' I asked.

'I don't know what to make of it. I trust in the Lord and I ask Father Ningonwe for his guidance, but I have to say I just don't know what to make of it.

59

'It doesn't surprise me that Mary would be different than the other women. You know, the ones who suffered so when the soldiers came through. It just makes sense that it would be different for Mary.

'I haven't seen her since all this happened. Since she had that child. And, oh, my dear Joseph. I can't figure him out. There's the miracle if you ask me. I don't know about any of the rest, but I think Joseph is the miracle. You don't see that often. Hardly ever. I've never heard of a story like it around here, of a man who did that. It's just not our culture for a man to do that. Even the best Christian men around here don't do that.

'You see, Mr. Masterson, in our culture when a man takes back a woman after that happens, he is the one who brings dishonor on himself. It's him the village blames. Joseph didn't even ask her to pay the bride price back, or ask her to make gifts to his family. Sometimes that's enough. He didn't ask her for anything in return. You don't see many men like that.'

* * *

I tried to find other people who knew Mary. I tried to get access to other family members. We found their houses but they all waved me away. I did not insist.

Then I asked my driver to take me to the tea estate where Joseph was the manager. It was a simple, one-story building of white stucco walls with green trim around the windows—neat, and functional. Inside there was a small waiting area with tea samples that was set up for the occasional visitor or buyer; I looked at the leaves, smelled them, and tried some tea. A salesperson, a young man in his mid-twenties dressed in well-pressed slacks, a white shirt, and a tie, received me, treating me as if I were a major buyer about to make a sizable deal with them. He waited on me and asked after every sip what I thought of the tea. He held out a simple metal tray to receive my cup and then he offered me another one, with a different tea blend.

His ritual seemed designed to make me move slowly. He insisted on explaining the picking process, and the growth cycle, and the characteristics of good tea.

Finally, when he paused for a breath, I asked him if I could meet Joseph. I explained that I was a journalist doing a story about Mary, and that I had written articles and a book about the conflicts in the region. I gave him my business card. He looked at me seriously, carefully examined my card, and then went into the next room that was separated by a single door from the main showroom.

He came back a few minutes later.

'I am so sorry, Mr. Masterson. He is busy.'

I thought I could sense someone standing just on the other side of the door. The assistant looked at me for a moment, awaiting my response.

'Okay. Thank you for your time. And for the tea.'

'Do come back if you're interested in buying any,' he said.

* * *

That evening I followed my routine of checking e-mails at the Internet café in town and then I returned to the guesthouse for dinner. Still I did not see Isabelle.

The next morning, Tuesday, I had breakfast earlier than

usual so I could reach Mary's house early. Again, Isabelle was not there.

I sat in the front seat with my driver. We drove past the tea estate again and through the fields and through Mary's village to where the line started. It was still early in the morning but there were already bicycles and minivans ahead of us and honking around the entrance.

I did not wait for my driver to park. He left me as close as he could to the entrance to the house compound and I gathered my backpack.

I greeted the women in front of the house in Swahili, introduced myself again and asked to see Mary's sister. I could not recall if this was one of the women I had already met.

'They told me to come back today.'

I sat down in a white plastic chair. The sun was not yet hot enough for me to need to move the chair to the shade. I simply sat and waited and tried to read but could not concentrate. It seemed like an hour or more but it could have been less. Finally, I heard a voice behind me.

'She will see you, Mr. Masterson. Mary will see you now.'

I followed the woman through the front gate of the house and to the side entrance. We were back at the small porch I had been on before. This time I saw that out back there were a few animals (goats, chickens, and beyond those, a few long-horned cattle). There were banana trees and a few mango trees, and some spindly papaya trees. I could see a neatly kept garden with tomato bushes and flowers and some other plants I couldn't identify.

They asked me to sit in a chair just outside the kitchen door.

It was then that I truly heard her voice for the first time.

Although I could not see her face, I had no doubt which was her voice. When Isabelle and I had been here briefly before, Mary had spoken only a few words while her staff did most of the talking. This time I clearly heard her voice.

I have described the faces and voices of warlords, gun smugglers, diamond peddlers, World Bank staff, child soldiers, pastors, and aid workers, and of European and American adventurers who don't seem to know there is a conflict going on in the region. But Mary defied my descriptive abilities.

Her voice sounded nasal at first, as if she had congested sinuses. But once I got used to that, I realized that beyond the nasal tone there was a softness with a depth of timbre and a fullness and presence that was extraordinary. Although I knew it was impolite, I stood up to watch her through the open doorway.

She was talking to someone but I didn't think it was a session or an audience or whatever you might call her visits. She looked at me through the door. She engaged my eyes. She was neither shy nor arrogant, but merely reserved, as if she didn't like being looked at. As if to say: *I tell what I want to tell. I show what I want to show. This I do, receive these lines of people, this I do because I have no choice.*

I wanted to let myself float in the timbre of that voice, a timbre that resonated in the comfort center of my brain. Of that I was convinced. I wanted to remain in its presence. I wanted to hear her talk. I wanted her to say more. Judging from the line outside, all of us did.

I put that description of Mary's voice in my notes, but Sam was not satisfied with it. I didn't know how else to describe her. I could have told him to make a list of soothing sounds and experiences. *Think of all the things that comfort you most, and that was Mary's voice and her presence.* A long shower with no shortage of water after driving ten hours in a hot car through parts of the Central African savannah. The first spoonful of food in the morning that your mother nudges toward you. The smell and feel of your grandmother's hand pressing your cheek. Your grandfather holding your hand as he walks you to your favorite park. A nipple to your infant lips when your brain is flooded with hunger messages. But I knew Sam would slash all of this. *I can't explain,* I would say.

I continued to watch Mary from afar. She moved slowly but did not seem weary; it seemed to be the pace at which life came to her. She flowed from one space to the next with a gentle, measured sway that matched her voice.

A few minutes later, the woman talking to Mary waved me in.

'Come in, Mr. Masterson,' Mary said in English, as I stood in the doorway.

A third woman, another assistant, I presumed, came inside the house along with me. The assistant stared at me, nodded, and pointed to a chair at the kitchen table. I could hear the muffled sound of a child crying in the distance.

'She prefers Swahili most of the time,' the assistant said to me. 'It is the language she feels that she can heal in and talk freely in. It is her mother tongue. It is necessary for these things. I will translate for you as needed.'

I nodded; although I speak reasonable Swahili, translation is useful for more complex conversations.

'So, you are a journalist,' Mary said in English, as Mary's sister, the assistant, and the interpreter looked at me suspiciously.

It was not a question but an affirmation.

'Yes. I've written about the conflicts in the region, a book on the Lord's Resistance Army, and I write articles for news magazines. I think it is important that other countries, Europe and the United States, know what has happened here.'

Mary was silent. I think she was looking in the direction of the crying child, as if waiting for the crying to recommence. Then she spoke to me, again in English.

'I have turned all journalists away. You never get it right when you talk to us. You do not believe our ways. You do not understand us.'

She let this hang in the air and I thought this might be a short meeting. Then she spoke again, even more slowly and calmly.

'I will let you interview me. But not because I want my story told.'

I nodded.

'Because you need this.'

She looked straight at me.

'You know why, don't you?'

Mary, the interpreter, her sister, and her assistant all stared at me. I felt as if they wanted some sort of confession from me. There was a moral weight to the question in the way Mary had asked it. I could think of a thousand things I had done, and yet none that made any sense right now, none that had anything to do with this interview. I was the *mzungu* with the jeep, the one with 'press' written on the side of it, the one with the famous book, the one with grants to come here and do this research, the *mzungu* who had articles published in leading news magazines. I needed this because this is what I do. Why else would I *need* this?

65

'Could we have about two hours?' I asked.

Mary gave me a soft smile, one that conveyed a look of patient amusement, one that showed her understanding that I was avoiding the topic she had brought up and registering to us all that she was allowing me to avoid it.

'You can't possibly know me in two hours.'

Again, she paused.

I was silent.

'I will see you in the afternoon tomorrow and the next days until you know my story. And then you will go and then you will tell it and I will talk to no more of you. You journalists. And you will have found what you need.'

I did not believe there would be enough of interest about her story that would warrant that much time, but I agreed. As I stood up to leave, I heard her say something in Swahili and then the translator rendered it into English.

'I am sorry to know about your father. I will pray for him. I will pray for him to be strong in this difficult moment. And for you.'

Here was the *pai-de-santo* yet again. Here was the hand smashing my head on the wall, a hand that had no way to find me, but did.

A dozen thoughts flew through my head, all of them asking how she could have known this. And every one of those thoughts ran into the same wall: she could *not* have known this.

'Thank you,' I said, genuinely touched by the concern.

As I walked out, I turned back for an instant and watched Mary flow into another part of the house.

* * *

And so began her story, told to me over ten days—a few hours a day or a few minutes—depending on the day. I agreed to her timetable. And every day, when I went to Mary's house, I was scrutinized by her assistants. I was reminded again of my interviews with Mai Mai commanders and all those young men standing around the gate and porches. As they searched me for weapons and looked me in the eye, I could tell that they wanted to, even if just in these few minutes, show me that *they*—not me, the *mzungu*—were in charge.

The looks on the faces of Mary's assistants asked: *Did you see how long the line is today? Who do you think you are? Do you think you are worthy? Do you know how many would give anything to be in your position?*

But Mary always seemed indifferent to these looks and comments. She invited me in with that voice—that mother's voice. With her, during the interviews, I was at home. Here I was at ease in my own skin even though I was the only *mzungu*, and, on most days, the only man.

* * *

Back at the guesthouse later that evening, Isabelle was seated in the dining area, reading a book. She smiled when she saw me, and I smiled back. She was wearing a simple black sleeveless dress and had a brightly colored woven shawl around her shoulders. It was a casual, elegant look that said, *I could go out or I could stay in.* I wanted to think she had dressed this way on the chance she would see me.

'Hey, how are you?' I asked.

'Fine, tired. I've been doing interviews and field visits non-stop. One of our most important donors was visiting. She finally left today. And you?'

'Fine. I met Mary today. We start the interviews tomorrow. She's given me a week. She says I need that long to know her story.'

Our eyes met for a moment, then she turned away. I did not tell her my impressions of Mary. I was afraid I would give away the confusion that was going on in my head.

'I'll share with you what I hear,' I said.

'Thank you,' she said, looking back at me. 'I think you can understand why her story is so important to us. My bosses in Geneva and New York are sending lots of messages asking what I have found out. They're dying to get a picture and interview of her on our website and in our reports.'

'Yes, of course.'

The staff from the guesthouse asked if we wanted dinner and I nodded, as did Isabelle.

'Do you mind if I ask you something?' I said. 'Please don't take this as an accusation, but did you tell anyone about what I told you about my father having cancer?'

Isabelle looked at me as if I had just accused her of a crime.

'No, I would never do that. You told me in confidence.'

She said *confidence* as the French version of the word; I had by now noticed that her pronunciation shifted sometimes.

I smiled, slightly embarrassed.

'Mary. At the end of the meeting. She told me she was sorry about my father. That she would pray for him. I hadn't said a thing about him.'

Isabelle's eyes got wider and she did not shield them this time. They were lovely, and were set off by her dark, full eyebrows. I thought her eyes changed shades of green slightly and that they were as puzzled as my own.

'How could she know?' she asked.

'No idea.'

I was silent while the woman from the guesthouse served our meal.

'I've heard dozens of stories since I've been in the region about miracles,' I continued, 'children or adults being brought back from the dead, terminal cancers cured, the same kind of stories I heard in Brazil. People who can talk to the dead or see things before they happen. Half the time, these are people with graduate degrees, I mean UN and government officials, university professors, who all swear it's as true as anything they have seen.'

'I have a Chilean grandmother from an educated family, all of them university-educated, and she and all of them believe the same things,' Isabelle said.

'So what is it? What does it mean?' I asked.

'Really good intuition?' Isabelle said. 'The ability to perceive things that are there but just below the surface? They used to call us witches, you know?'

'Yeah, well, that still happens here,' I said. 'It doesn't end well when it does.'

'Of course. Women who can perceive these things frighten us. *We* frighten you men by sensing these things.'

'For sure,' I said, smiling.

'Okay,' I continued, 'here's my theory. We know that historically women were denied education, and access to the sciences.

You couldn't be doctors or scientists, so you used knowledge from nature. You figured out things by learning from nature and daily life and, yeah, well, the religious leaders and scientists, all men, of course, found women dangerous. Right? That part we know.'

'Right,' she said.

'Okay, so we can take that further. In evolutionary terms, women who could read the intentions of others, I mean perceive things just below the surface, would be safer. They would be more likely to survive, right? So, maybe it's just that women are more intuitive because it serves an evolutionary function.'

Isabelle smiled.

'That's your rational argument,' she said. 'But what do you think about Mary? Does she really know something about you?'

'I'll call it luck this time. I'll tell you if it happens again. Two or three times will be a trend and then I'll get worried.'

We ate our dinner in silence for a few minutes, and I think Isabelle could tell that I did not really know how to answer that question.

'You were going to show me your father's pictures. The famous one you talked about.'

I nodded; she *was* intuitive. She realized that I had a safety zone, and she was figuring out how to get beyond it.

I opened my laptop.

* * *

His famous picture had been published in newspapers and magazines, on covers, in full two-page spreads, and in 'year in review' editions of major news magazines. *It was an example of what black and white photojournalism could do*, journalism professors said. The gray of the soldiers' uniforms, the early morning light that created ample contrast, the shadows that hinted at dark things going on, the pale, translucent purity of the girl's skin, the eyes alert and mouths caught in motion. It was a hideous moment captured for posterity. The viewer, while looking, was inside the war.

It is mostly a photo of dangerous, laughing men. There is one who is closer to us, closer to the foreground. He has the biggest smile. He is laughing and talking, we presume to one of the other men, or to all of them. He is slightly taller than the rest, or made to seem so by the angle of the photo. The direction of his head, the way it thrusts upward, suggests that he is in charge. He has receding dark hair, a large, Roman nose, and slightly droopy eyelids over vivid, alert eyes. We can almost hear his voice barking in Serbo-Croatian. He has a cigarette in one hand, and is pushing or holding the girl with the other.

Some captions called her 'a girl,' others 'a young woman.' Her face is slightly hidden. She has a soldier's overcoat around her, and in the shadow below her chin and neck, just before where we might see cleavage, it is apparent that she is wearing nothing under the coat. Her skin, just above her breasts, is painfully, vulnerably, soft, white, and smooth. For a moment our eyes are lost there. We think of the classic alabaster statues of women with impossibly perfect skin, or of the peach-fuzz teenage girls and boys we once were or once kissed. Whichever it is, our eyes, involuntarily, look there, rest there, dream there.

She is looking at us through hair that partially covers her eyes. But there is no mistake that she is looking at us. Her eyes call for help, but at the same time tell us that she does not believe that help will come. In one description of the photo the girl's eyes are called 'enigmatic' and the photo as 'simultaneously repulsing us and calling us to act, to take a stand against this.'

We all know what has happened to her, and what may happen again. And some of us, as we looked—whether repulsed or called to action—wondered why and how we got to see this. How could these men be looking on, laughing, knowing we are looking, knowing they will suffer no sanctions, knowing that we—the viewers, and the photographer—pose no threat? We have come this close and done nothing. The laughing Bosnian-Serb soldiers know this; the girl knows this.

The questions came slowly. At first the journalists were focusing their articles on the shift in the war, NATO involvement, the peace treaty in the works, uncovering the extent of the ethnic cleansing and all that came with it. But when the articles about the war had run their course there were the stories about the journalists who covered the war, and the big publications wanted the Lyndon Masterson story.

They usually sent women to interview him. My father was suitably charming, not classically handsome, but rugged, intense, a chain-smoker, disarming in his wrinkled khakis, light blue dress shirts, and well-traveled, brown leather jacket. It took me many years to understand that it was a uniform that told us—and the women sent to interview him—that he was more interested in other things than the way he dressed. He was interested in the photo, the moment, the chase; let other men worry about having their shirts pressed.

I witnessed one of these interviews. Others I saw on TV or in magazines.

The women journalists asked questions; some batted their eyes.

Why does she see no help arriving? What did he, the photographer, do afterwards? How did he, the photographer, get there, into the Bosnian-Serb camp? Could he have done anything?

His answers were always vague.

'Photographers photograph. The good ones get in the heart of it, they get inside.'

Once, in the *Playboy* interview, he went further.

'We are like puppeteers. The good ones, dressed in black, cease to exist.

'You don't see them. The audience, in this case the subject, stops remembering that a photographer is there. And the viewer forgets about the photographer as well. You don't see us. You see only the photograph, that moment. You become the photographer. The separation between the photo and photographer breaks down and you are there.'

Inevitably they asked: *What happened to her?*

'Armed extremists carrying out ethnic cleansing held her. Bosnian and Croatian troops couldn't get there, but I believed this needed to be seen.'

'But you knew—or had a pretty good idea—of what would happen to the girl?'

'I knew what was already happening to her. And I knew what would happen to more women, to her sisters, if we didn't get this information out.'

'But could you have helped her? Could you have rescued her?'

Some years later, I would compare the various responses my father gave to that question.

Bosniak troops fired rounds in our direction a few moments later and we scattered.

A land mine went off, some soldiers went to investigate, and I took advantage of the confusion to take the picture and slip away.

The commanding officer saw me taking the picture and ordered the men back to their barracks and told me to leave.

Sometimes my father mentioned just one of these, sometimes two of the three, sometimes all three. I could never tell if they were contradictory, complementary, or mutually exclusive.

* * *

'You've spent a lot of time thinking about that picture,' Isabelle said.

'I think I know more about that photo than I do about him,' I said.

'It meant something, though,' she said. 'It accomplished something. And it is beautiful and shocking and human all at the same time.'

I shrugged, and rubbed my hand across my mouth.

'You won't be upset if I tell you that it's a lot like what you do,' she said. 'I know you said you don't want to be like him.'

'It's the not the same, though.'

'No, but you're trying to do something similar even if your methods are different.'

I closed my laptop. I didn't want to respond to that. I was increasingly intrigued by her and equally frightened. If I had been brave enough, I would have said this: *I don't give a fuck about that picture.* He was away from us and he was torturing my mother to get it. And he left that girl there. How could he leave her behind? What political outcome was justified by that? How could he look at all that was happening around him, and at her, and leave her behind? And leave *us* behind.

INTERVIEW 1 — MARY OF KIVU

[Note to reader: I have rendered Mary's account as translated to me from Swahili with minimal editing.]

I will start at the beginning so you know it all, so you know my story.

You know Kivu, eh? You will know what I mean then.

The nights there, they are soft. There may be the creaking of bugs, maybe music in the background if someone is having a party, or maybe it is coming from a bar.

And there is always a breeze. We have lightening, but most of the time even our thunder is soft. Soft rumbles beyond the mountains.

We are lucky. Blessed. If not for the wars. If not for those men. If not for the hearts of men turned sour and angry and full of hate that they do not even understand. Men following the orders of other men. Lost men. Very lost men.

If not for them, Kivu is where God would come to rest.

Do you know the story of Lake Kivu? No?

Way before, long, long ago, here was all dry, hot and dry, all hard work. The people could barely grow enough to eat. It was not this green you see today.

People competed with each other for any little thing, even for food. No one helped each other. Everyone had small, small plots of land and kept to themselves.

But one man was very kind. He had some crops left over so he would share with those who couldn't grow enough to keep themselves fed. But his wife was selfish and did not like this. She would yell at him every day: 'Why do you give away our crops when we have so little?'

But this man kept giving away. He was a very good man.

God saw his deeds and so He gave him a magic cow. This cow gave milk, beans, peas, cassava, all the food they needed. But God told the man not to tell anyone about the magic cow. He said: 'Just give this to your wife so she will leave you in peace.'

One day, the man was called to the king's court, the *Mwami*. The kind man asked God what he should do with the magic cow while he was away. God told him to give it to his wife to milk in the meantime, but God said that she had to keep it secret.

So while the husband was away, the wife—the silly, young wife—invited a young man to visit her. The young man searched the house and saw all their food and wondered how it was that this woman and her husband had so much. The young man looked at the cow and he looked in the cupboards but saw nothing to give it away. But he was determined to make the wife tell him the secret. Aw, young wives are so weak!

She gave him the information. She milked the magic cow in front of the young man and he saw all those kinds of food coming from it. Then he leapt up, ran to the village, and told everyone about it. He yelled in every corner: 'We no longer need to work! We will have enough to eat, all of us! We never have to work again! They have been hiding this from us!'

Of course, God saw all of this and was not happy. That very night He punished the wife. When the wife went to go pee before she went to bed, her pee did not stop. She peed and peed and peed and it did not stop. Her pee filled the land, as far as you can see, the trees, her house, her barn, everything. Her house broke apart and become islands floating in the pee. There was so much that she too was washed away in her own pee.

When the husband came back, he saw the immense lake. He had no house, no wife, but he had a sweet, sweet lake at the edge of his land. And it was filled with all the crops he could want.

Now we have birds, we have fish, we have coffee and tea and fruit trees and we have all this green and we have all these crops that came from that magic cow sent to us by God.

That is our Kivu Eve. Always a woman, eh!

[Mary giggled at this.]

And so Lake Kivu came to be. Her pee was so sweet and there was so much of it that it made a lake, the most beautiful in all of Africa. Eh, in all the world.

Kivu is my home. My sweet pee lake.

* * *

I was raised here—a sister, a daughter, a schoolgirl, a wife, and now a mother. Three sisters like me. My father always said he was blessed to have four daughters, a marvelous one, a fantastic one, a wonderful one, and a beautiful one. I am the one he called beautiful. Many fathers were not happy to have daughters but my father was.

I dreamed from when I was a little girl of a man who would protect me, love me. Because a girl loved by her father will only have a man who loves her so.

I adored my school uniform. I was so proud of it—that pink blouse and the skirt. I would wash it and iron it a second time if my mother or the housegirl didn't do a good job. And I studied. I was so serious.

The older women told us how to stretch ourselves.

[The translator stopped for a moment when Mary started to tell this part. I could tell there was something about it that bothered her.]

How to stretch our vaginas and showed us which plants to rub there so it wouldn't hurt. This would give our husbands more pleasure, they told us. We had heard from the other girls that it would make us more sensitive too, give us pleasure.

[Mary smiled as she said this and looked away from me in shyness.]

Although it didn't seem to me that you needed to do much more to that part to make it more sensitive.

School was the most important thing to me. I would stay awake worried sick the night before a test. I would cry if I did not get the best marks.

'Mary, Mary, she only studies. So serious. When you gonna smile, Mary? When you gonna come out and play, Mary? So much more to life than your books, Miss Mary the schoolgirl.'

That's what they said to me. The boys and the men. My father would chase them away like you might a stray dog. He didn't take them seriously. Or maybe he did. *Shoo, shoo,* he said to them. And then he said to me: *Come inside, Mary.*

* * *

It was a teacher at school. Miss Unygire. She introduced me to poetry. And it was all I wanted to read. Do you like poetry? We had classes in English and in French.

80

And you must know about my dear Joseph.

He was from a nearby village, closer to the city by the lake. He went to the boys' school that was across the way from ours, from the girls' school.

I had seen him as a little boy because we went to the same church. I thought of him as a small, small boy. He was quiet and had a proud face. But he was a small, small boy who liked to read like me. I wondered if he had the same strong thoughts I had about what I read. But he was too small, too frail for me to take him seriously, eh. He could not be the one I was waiting for, the one I was stretching myself for, the one I would give pleasure and who would give pleasure to me.

Then one day, just like that, from one day to the next it seemed, he was all filled out. This book boy, a small child like me who kept to himself, had become a strong young man. His arms, they did shine. I remember looking at the way he bent his arms and watching that muscle move, on the back of his arm. This was a new kind of poetry to me.

[As she said this M. laughed the same free-spirited laugh as that woman in the wheelchair, and looked momentarily at the floor.]

I sat under the tree between our two schools. It was the yard where we played. I sat under that tree hoping he would see me, that he would look at me. But he looked right through me. He did not see me. I looked at myself and thought it must be the same for him. I was a small, small girl with nothing to attract him. No breasts, no hips, nothing to show the outside world, to show him, that I was becoming a woman.

I could not make him look into my eyes. I thought if he saw them, if he truly saw them, he would see how I felt and he would know me and he would feel like I did.

So I would sit under that tree, reading my poetry and stories and studying. When other boys tried to talk to me, I would ignore them. They did not exist, just as I did not exist for Joseph.

The boys' school only went up to year 8, so Joseph and the boys who stayed in school, whose parents could keep them in school, had to go away to the city by the lake for secondary school. So Joseph stopped coming everyday. I would see him sometimes in church, but always from far away. And then he stopped coming to church.

I imagined that he was with a girl—no, with a woman. I imagined that she had big hips and large breasts and the straightest hair or maybe she had beautiful braids and beautiful clothes and that she came from the city. I imagined that she had stretched herself well and would be very desirable for a man.

I imagined that he was walking with her along the lake, that he was taking her on a boat ride. That he hired a fisherman to take them across the lake to one of the islands. And I imagined that he was taking this girl to sit on the shore of the island and look at the sky, and that he was telling her how beautiful she was.

Eh, the silly things in girls' heads.

'My silly Mary,' he told me later when I told him this. 'I was walking with the cows and I was not reading poetry to anyone. Not even to myself. I was reading for mathematics.'

My dear Joseph studied and studied. His family was working to save money so they could send him to the university. He passed his entrance exams and his family and other families in the church put together the money to send him there. My family was not close to his so we didn't help, but we knew some who did.

A boy from a nearby village going to university! This was reason for celebration.

But I was not part of the celebration. I was just the little girl with no breasts and no hips sitting under the tree reading her books and dreaming of a man who would take her on a boat to see the islands in Lake Kivu.

* * *

That was when we began to hear the stories. There had always been stories. About the lost men. The men who would drink their magic drinks to keep the bullets away, men who they said could see in the dark. Men who had a magic potion that made bullets turn into water when they hit their bodies. Men who could come at any time and attack those who didn't help them, or who might attack even if you did help them. Men who did horrible things to women and girls, who took girls away to be their bush wives. But it always seemed so far away from us, so many mountains away, so many lakes and volcanoes away.

Now the stories were coming from closer. Then there were stories of the men, eh, the boys too, who had formed new armies that would attack anyone who was not from their group. We heard of things in villages nearby. Now it was only one mountain away. My parents would tell of these things in quiet voices in their bedroom when they thought we could not hear them, just as they thought we did not hear them when they made love.

I remember I heard my father say that he was glad that he did not have any sons, because these men, or the government soldiers, would come and take away his sons and turn them into killers.

These stories frightened me. I read more and more, read from my books about places far away, books that told stories that had nothing to do with the fighting and killing that was now just a village away. And when I was scared for our village, I would keep myself calm by thinking that it was good that Joseph would be going away to university in Uganda.

I believed that his books and all his studying would keep him safe. That would be his shield.

But at university, I thought, he would also be away from me. He would not see me turn into a woman.

And you know what happened? I was reading poetry and stories every day after school, every book I could find. I thought every book, every poem was written just for me, about me. I was amazed at these feelings put into words that these writers and poets wrote.

And then one day I felt the blood, the monthly blood. An auntie had told me about it. I knew something about it. But I was convinced at first that it was the poetry that brought it on. I like to think that poetry made me become a woman, eh.

I like that thought.

I was happy when that happened. It meant that I was becoming a woman. I thought I could get my Joseph's attention.

I could not stop worrying about what would happen when he left. Away at university, he would be around all those other girls, those city girls. They knew things we did not. They did things we did not. They were not like us respectable girls from Kivu—us plain, respectable girls. I was sure that once he left our village and met those girls, he would never come back. And he would never be mine.

* * *

So, you see, it was just a few weeks before he went to Uganda for university. He had been to Goma and come back, making his arrangements for starting his classes.

I was sitting in one of my usual spots, on the grass under a tree near the school yard. I had gone from poetry to novels. Books were not easy to get. They were expensive and hard to find outside the city, and by the time they made it to our village they would sometimes be missing the cover, and if you were unlucky, some pages.

I had a worn copy of *The Plague* that was missing the last pages. The front cover was still on it, but the back cover and some of the last pages were lost. Still, I had read it three times already. To me, the story ended before Dr. Rieux's wife died. Before he received the telegram telling him that she had died. My version ended with that moment of the plague having passed through the worst stage and we believe it will get better and we think that his hard work and bravery will see him through. That he will be rewarded.

Even though it was my third time reading it, I was so engrossed that I did not see Joseph coming up, or maybe I just wanted to make it look that way.

[Mary giggled.]

'I didn't expect that his wife would die, did you?' he said.

I looked at him for a moment, both stunned, and saddened, as if a truth and hope I believed in had been pulled away, but also thinking that, of course, how could it end any other way? How could I be so silly as to think it would come out okay for him, that he could labor and see the death around him but come out with everything fine? I turned my copy toward him and he saw that it was missing the back cover and some pages.

'You didn't have that part? That's what happens to the books that make it out here.'

I just looked at him. I was making sense of the story now, looking back at the cover, so absorbed in this new ending, and so sure that Joseph was not interested in me that I knew he would be walking away. He was not, for the moment, what interested me. I was saddened by this story, feeling sorry for Dr. Rieux, imagining his face and what meaning life would now have to him, left only with his pestering mother and his memories of all who had died, of all those he had tended to but could not save.

I barely noticed when Joseph spoke again.

'Your hair. And your dress. You look different.'

I had braids now and my face took on a different look, and I had started to fill out although I had some growing still to do. But I had breasts. It was a new dress. But what he noticed, I think, was that my dress now fit me in a different way.

I looked up at him.

'I thought about you when I was in Goma,' he said. 'I was in the bookshop.

It's near the university. It's where the students buy their supplies and it's a whole store, bigger than any near here, and it's full of books. They must have thought I looked like a countryside boy with my mouth open looking at it all. And I thought of you and I knew you would feel the same way. They tell me Kampala has even bigger bookstores.'

I just looked at him.

'I brought you a book,' he said, holding out a wrapped package for me.

I took it, looking at him. It was not often that I had a brand new book that hadn't been passed around through many hands.

'To help with my education,' I said, with a bit of scorn. 'For little Mary who likes books and is stuck in Kivu and can't get them.'

'No, Mary, because I like you. Because I thought you might smile when you saw it and because ... well, it's a love story.'

He paused. I think he was nervous. And then he continued.

'When you smile, you are the prettiest girl in all of Kivu.'

I opened the package. It was *Love in the Time of Cholera*, by Gabriel Garcia-Marquez. I had heard of him but had never been able to get one of his books.

'Thank you,' I said, working to keep my voice calm and still.

'I didn't know you were reading *The Plague*. Anyway, there is disease, but the ending is much different.'

He paused and looked away. I was still making sense of this new Joseph, of this new way he looked at me.

'I'll be going to Uganda in a month, you know. I wanted to talk to you ... Before I left.'

In my head, at that moment, the world changed colors. I knew that foods would have different flavors. Music would sound different. Even my sisters would be less annoying. God and all his angels were real. Everything was different. And he was mine. I knew it right then. He was mine.

* * *

[Mary took a break to tend to her child and returned a few minutes later.]

So, my Joseph. Yes.

But, oh, how the Lord works, eh, how he plays with the hearts of silly girls, especially in Kivu.

You see, I met his brother, Edouard, at about the same time.

His brother was trouble on two feet, a lost man, but the kind that women and girls think is their job to help him find himself, to

87

fix him, and to hold him down. We all think we can make men like him right. He was a man who could look at you with the force of a poem, whose eyes told you what he wanted and made you want it back.

[I could not make out the sound Mary made as she mentioned Edouard for the first time. I thought at first it was one of the giggles she used when she talked about sex or intimacy. But this laugh was different. And then she switched to English for the first time. She spoke it slowly and deliberately.]

He is a bad man. A bad man in the good way, if you know what I mean. And a bad man in the bad way at the same time.

[She paused again here and continued in English.]

And now I must look after my baby. You come back tomorrow. I will tell you about Edouard and about what happened when my Joseph was away at university in Uganda.

SEVEN

As I left the first interview, I saw women in the line outside arguing. Their voices were raised and they looked at each other and then at the ground. This was not like West Africa, or New York, where women's raised voices were commonplace. Women here are usually subdued. After all the wars, past and present, silence is the prevailing mode for women (and for most men).

My driver came up to me.

'What is happening?' I asked.

He smiled.

'This one,' he said, pointing to one of the women, 'said the other one stole her husband. And this one said that the first woman, his wife, made a penis grow out of the man's head.'

He saw my puzzled look.

'She says that the first woman, the one who said she is the wife, put a curse on the man, her husband, and made his penis go from here to his head.'

'It must be true,' my driver continued. 'I have seen these things before. A woman who got pregnant in her sleep from a man who secretly loves her. A man who finds the smell of a woman in his bed even though he knows she is far from him and with another man. These things happen.'

I nodded. Here were these stories again. I never knew how to respond. Here were people—in this case my driver, whom I trusted with my life—swearing by the existence of supernatural happenings. It was as if he—they—could see into a parallel universe where the laws of physics and nature don't apply, a universe that he swore was right in front of us. All I could do was nod.

'And what do they want from Mary?' I asked.

'The one who wants the man, the second wife, wants Mary to restore the man to the way he was.'

'I think I would want that too,' I said.

My driver laughed.

We walked to the car and he began driving me back to the guesthouse. Before we arrived, I asked him to take me directly to the cybercafe again. I did not feel like seeing Isabelle just yet.

Once we arrived at the cybercafe and I was connected, I looked at a few medical sites on esophageal cancer, and then I looked at my e-mails.

There was one from my uncle Randall. 'An update on your father.'

Before I could open the message, the power in the cybercafe went out. The young African man with a Penn State T-shirt and jeans at the front of the café came and told me not to worry, that it would come back on in a few minutes. I nodded and looked back at my laptop. I thought about waiting, but I was hungry and tired.

I could hear a generator come on in the distance and then I saw that the Lebanese grocery store across the street had its lights on, so I closed my laptop, paid for my Internet use, and walked across the street to the store. I bought a bottle of South African red wine that I knew was drinkable. I wanted to sleep. I knew I was going to have trouble sleeping. I returned to my car and asked my driver to take me back to the guesthouse.

* * *

This is what I thought about that night when I could not sleep: my father. Once when I was visiting him in New York, he had left me alone in his apartment. While he was gone, I began looking through the boxes of photos he had in his study. Some of them were gruesome. There was a photo he had taken of necklacing in South Africa, putting a tire filled with gasoline around the victim and setting it on fire. The man's face is writhing in pain and onlookers are cheering.

There were pictures of my father with women in various countries.

In one picture, my father is standing next to a beautiful, young African woman with skin the earthy brown color of vanilla beans. One of the pictures is badly discolored, as if it had been burned, or overexposed—or ripped out of a camera without being rewound into its canister.

There was a picture of my father in Sri Lanka, with the Tamil rebel leaders he was photographing, and another of him at a beach, a young woman next to him, this time Asian. The green foliage behind them seems to be creeping in all directions, stopped only by the thin line of sand before the ocean starts. Their arms are touching. Her skin is the color of copper, and I can see my father looking toward the young woman's mouth and her coffee-with-milk colored lips.

I thought about the time he spent with these women, investing himself, making himself charming, while he came home and showed indifference to my mother and me.

At the bottom of the pile in one of the boxes were his pictures from Bosnia. First there was a picture of soldiers eating, and drinking wine straight out of a bottle. Then there was a picture of guards in a prison camp, their hands seeming to reach for the camera, but not in an aggressive way; their gaze was friendly. And there was a picture of my father having a drink out of the same bottle of wine with the soldiers. In one of the last pictures I saw, I could make out the officer who is in the center of the famous picture. My father is toasting in the officer's direction and both of them are laughing.

Later that same day, my father had a small party at his apartment for some journalist colleagues. They were all pleased to know that I was studying journalism and they all had advice for me.

With a cigarette in one hand, my father opened bottle after bottle of Macedonian wine for his journalist friends.

'Don't tell them this stuff cost me five dollars a bottle,' he winked at me.

INTERVIEW 2 – MARY OF KIVU

I was going to tell you about Edouard and about the time Joseph and I spent apart. You have been in love; I think you will understand me.

[Mary looked at me with serious eyes before she continued.]

Before Joseph left, we had long walks together. We talked for hours.

Well, hours were difficult to have because my family would always be nearby, or they would send one of my sisters to fetch me.

Once, though, Joseph and I managed to get away for a longer time. It was a Sunday. He took me on a boat ride on the lake. I don't know how he afforded that. Maybe he took some of his university money. We silly girls don't stop to think about that, do we?

We stopped on some of the islands and he would help me step out of the boat to keep my dress dry. I remember feeling his hands on me when he helped me down or when I nearly tripped once, and he held me steadily in his arms.

We watched the swimming cows pulling boats.

[Mary looked up at me with a slight smile waiting for my reaction.]

Have you seen the swimming cows?

[I nodded and smiled back. She wanted to tell me anyway.]

Mzungus never believe it is possible, but cows can swim. And in

Kivu sometimes they pull the canoes or boats for the men. Just the tops of their heads and their noses are out of the water.

On the way back to the dock in the boat, Joseph read me a poem. It was 'Ode to a Grecian Urn,' by John Keats.

> *Fair youth, beneath the trees, thou canst not leave*
> *Thy song, nor ever can those trees be bare;*
> *Bold Lover, never, never canst thou kiss,*
> *Though winning near the goal—yet, do not grieve;*
> *She cannot fade, though thou hast not thy bliss,*
> *For ever wilt thou love, and she be fair!*

'I want this moment with you on my urn,' I told him. 'I want it to stay like this, just like this, until you come back.'

'I want this and every moment in my life to be on the urn,' he said.

I kissed him gently, but quickly, since it wouldn't have been appropriate for the boat pilot to see this.

As we approached the dock, I could see my father waiting. Joseph kept holding my hand, but I could not feel comfortable holding his hand with my father watching us like that.

When the boat pulled up, my father just waited. He did not run up to the boat. Joseph helped me out and then he went over to my father.

'Sir, I am Joseph Kirezi and I … ' he started, with his hand held out to my father.

My father ignored him and looked to me and said: 'What are you doing here? Alone with this boy? You told your mother you would be at church.'

I looked down at the ground.

'Sir, it was my idea. You see, I will be going way to university soon and I wanted to spend some time with your daughter.'

My father looked at Joseph but he said nothing.

'Go to church now,' he said to me, 'like you said you would.'

My father turned and started walking away saying nothing else. I looked up at Joseph, my head tilted to the ground, and I followed my father, staying several steps behind him. He did not say a thing to me on the way there. I wondered when I would see Joseph again.

I walked behind my father into the church and was miserable the rest of the mass. I wanted to run out and find Joseph. My mother gave me a stare that told me of the trouble I would have when I got home. My sisters looked at me and gave me hidden smiles.

'You shame me, daughter,' my mother said quietly to me as we walked out of church.

I could not believe what happened next.

There he was, waiting outside the church, in the place where the priest usually stood. My Joseph.

He came up to my father, my mother just behind them.

'Sir and Madam. I do not wish to be disrespectful. I apologize that we left without telling you where we were. Especially with the things that are happening around here. I understand why you are upset. I assure you, nothing happened. I am going away to university in Uganda soon and I want to spend time with your daughter. I was reading to her from a book of poems.

'I only have a few more days before I go away to university, but I hoped you would give me permission to let me call on your daughter in your house. So that she and I could read more poetry together.'

My father could not fathom how to respond to this, and, though

I wanted to, I dared not smile. I don't know if it was my father or me who was more impressed by this boy. My father just scowled at him and began walking in the direction of our house.

Joseph came over in the early evening for the next few days. Sometimes he had already eaten his dinner, but he always pretended he was hungry and at least ate something.

'I'm going away tomorrow,' he said one evening. 'But I wanted to know if you would wait for me.'

He gave me a book of poetry by Emily Dickinson.

My parents were not at home then. My sisters were watching but pretending they were not.

'I'll walk you back to the road,' I told Joseph, turning to look sternly at my sisters so they knew they should not follow me.

Once outside the house, he put his hand in mine and I leaned my head on his shoulder. We were both quiet and both so full of feelings.

Just before we got to where the road connected up to the main road, Joseph stopped and turned to me.

[Mary smiled at me and then looked at the ground.]

If he had asked me right then, I think I would have made love with him right there, right then, in the bush. Eh, silly girl that I was.

We said we would write each other, but we both knew how unreliable the postal service was, with the conflicts and all.

So my Joseph went away. He didn't know if he would have enough money to visit during holidays, so we did not know when we would see each other again. I did my best not to cry as he left.

My life went back to what it was before. I was studying every day, and then reading under the same tree. Only now, I did it to think of Joseph. I read and reread the Emily Dickinson poems. I was

96

sure her words said exactly what I felt.

It was not even a week after Joseph left when Edouard came by the tree where I was reading. Every time I saw him, he had a different girl on his arm, girls who did not mind showing that they were on his arm. Girls who had hips like I wanted. Before that day, he had always smiled at me but had never talked to me. Now he talked.

'Hi, sister-in-law,' he said.

The girl on his arm laughed at this.

'It is my job to watch you, little Mary,' he said.

Nearly every day he would say this and depending on the girl, she might laugh or she might leer at me. A few months passed.

My Joseph had by now been away for a long time, or at least it felt like a long time. I had no news from him. No letters. I knew he would have tried to write if letters would get through, but Uganda was a long way away. I would ask my father occasionally if he knew someone who was going there who could take a letter. He looked at me as if I were a silly little girl asking him to bring a dead butterfly back to life.

I kept studying and studying. I had in my mind that if I studied enough I would get to leave too, and I would get to university in Uganda and then Joseph and I would be back together. My secondary school went two years longer than most secondary schools, so I could stay there and study to be a teacher. I knew my family would not have enough money to send me to university, so I would finish teacher training. If all went well for me and for Joseph, he would return to Kivu at the time I was finishing my teacher training.

And then one day, many months after Joseph had gone away, Edouard walked by alone.

He sat down on the ground next to me. He told me to come to a wedding party with him.

'You can get some ideas for yours,' he said.

'Do you have news from Joseph?' I asked.

'He is fine, studying hard, and busy with his friends there. He says there are lots of girls there too. You know what the big city is like. You know about big city girls. You give them a ride. You buy them some food. You know what happens.'

He smiled. It was his dangerous smile.

'He told me to watch over you,' he said.

Back then Edouard was so proud of himself. He walked like his whole life had promise, like we did not live in a country with wars and battles and killing happening around us and all this poverty. He walked like the whole world was his and his life would get better every day. He stood tall, with his chest out. He played soccer. He wore those tight-fitting European shirts before the rest of the boys did. I don't know where he got them, because I know his family did not have much money, but he always had nice clothes.

After that I did not see Edouard for some time. I think he was working somewhere to help out with things at home. I missed Joseph terribly, but every time those ideas that Edouard put in my head came back, those images of other girls with my Joseph, I would try to remember the day on the lake and the day he held my hand as we walked to the road. Some nights, though, I would wake up in a panic that I could not remember Joseph's face, and I would only fall back to sleep once I could.

Then one day Edouard came alone again and found me reading and doing my schoolwork under my favorite tree.

'You have been looking too lonely and sad, my sister-in-law,' he said. 'You must come to the wedding party with me.'

I pretended I wasn't interested, but of course I was. I said no a few times and then I agreed to meet him at the wedding party. It was a girl my parents knew, and I told them and I was going on my own.

When I saw him at the wedding party, I said to him: 'I can't believe you're here alone. At a wedding. Eh.'

'I have to protect you,' he said.

'I can do that by myself.'

He made a kind of snort and then gave me that dangerous smile.

We danced a few dances, always in a big group. You know how we dance, right, Mr. Masterson? Here we cannot dance without moving our hips this way and that. Dancing for us is serious business. And for Edouard it was very serious. He knows how to dance and soon everyone was watching us.

In between dances, he would go off and drink a beer, a banana beer or a regular beer. But he never had too much. Some of the guys were having a lot and they were talking loudly but Edouard, no. He knew how to drink.

'Why don't you offer me one?' I asked.

He looked at me with and raised an eyebrow.

'Don't look at me that way. Girls can drink too. What of it?' I told him.

'I'm supposed to be watching over you,' he said.

'Joseph knows I don't need anyone to watch over me. You are here because you want to be here, not because he told you anything.'

He looked at me and then he went and got two beers and brought them back.

We danced again, and I had more beers. I had never had more than two.

And this time I had five. It was getting late. The lights were being turned out as if it was time to go, but we all knew what happened at these hours.

Edouard grabbed me, gently, and pulled me to him.

'You are right. I am here because I want to be. And I didn't come with any other girl because I didn't want to,' he said.

I did not pull away.

'And you are here because you wanted to come,' he said. 'You could have stayed at home thinking about Joseph.'

I looked at the ground. My head was spinning. Aw, silly young girls. Of course we want the Edouards. Of course we know what the Edouards want. We have to pretend that we don't. We have to pretend that we don't know what will happen and we have to pretend that we don't want it too. Eh.

[Mary was silent for a moment as if she was not sure she should tell me more.]

As he pulled me to him, I could feel his strength. And I could feel what he wanted. I did not stop him at first. His smell and his body and him whispering in my ears, those words that I could no longer understand and didn't want to.

[Now Mary looked at me, this time as if wanting to know if she could trust me, as if wanting to know if I understood. I looked back at her intensely.]

We went behind the school. I let him lead me there. He kept whispering to me how much he cared about me, how I could be his woman, that I was the most beautiful girl in the village. That none of those other girls meant a thing. That he would take care of me, take me anywhere I wanted to go in the whole world. I don't know if he said all these things or if I just wanted to believe that is what he was saying.

He found a wrapper hanging on a clothesline and put it on the ground near the school wall, in a place that did not face any houses. He was staring at me and I returned his stare.

I remember thinking about the poem, the one Joseph had read to me, 'Ode to a Grecian Urn.' Is this the moment I want on my urn, the moment of my youth, the moment to remember?

As I was thinking that and, at the same time feeling desire in my body, we heard the gunshots. Around Kivu men do not hunt with guns. They do not have guns. So when we hear gunshots we know what it means and our blood stops.

I was no longer thinking of Edouard or how he made me feel.

We heard shouting and screaming, and the voices of women and girls and men yelling. I would have screamed but I knew I couldn't. We didn't know if it was the government soldiers or one of the rebel groups. We knew what happened when these men and boys came into town. My heart was beating like it would explode. Edouard whispered to me that we should stay where we were or find a way to get inside the school.

'No, take me home. I want to be home.'

'It is safer here. They will not expect anyone to be here.'

'Take me to my house.'

He stared at me and I could see the fear in his eyes. I said that I would go home by myself if he did not take me. He looked at me with anger in his eyes. I thought for a moment that he might strike me. We heard more gunshots and more screams.

He looked away and then we heard that the movement was going the opposite direction. We did not talk on the way and I did not let him put his arm around me. We moved in the darkness, praying the soldiers would not come our direction.

When I got home my mother was crying that it was starting

again, that it was all starting again. My sisters were crying too, and my father was telling them all to stay calm and not to make any noise. But I could tell by his face that he was frightened too. I remember thinking I was glad that my Joseph was away, that he was safe in Uganda.

None of us slept that night. Every noise and every voice stirred us.

A few days later, when all seemed calm again, or at least, we thought it was, I was sitting under the tree reading. It was toward the end of the day and the sun was going down. Edouard came up and sat next to me.

'We can go for a walk,' he said. 'I know a quiet place where we can be alone.'

'No, Edouard. I like you. I do. But I'm confused. I have been waiting for Joseph for so long. I need to think.'

He stared at me. His eyes went from that king-of-the-world look to being so cold toward me that I was frightened. I did not know what to think, or what I wanted. And then his eyes softened again.

'There is no hurry, Mary.'

He touched my hand and then stood up to leave.

'It will be okay. The village is safe now. The rebels have gone away. I will wait as long as you need, sweet Mary. Now go on home. And dream of me like I will dream of you.'

Oh, how the boys and the men tell us lies.

And how confusing these things are for girls. Was my Joseph going out with sexy Ugandan girls in the city? Was he lonely and doing what boys do? Did he have friends who maybe had some extra money and took him dancing at those places in the city? Some nights I would cry myself to sleep. And some nights I would think of Edouard. I am ashamed to say that I found myself thinking of Joseph less and less.

[There was a baby's cry in the background and Mary looked up. I had noticed earlier that she looked tired.]

I must go, Mr. Masterson. My son is not sleeping well. I think it is more teeth coming in. You come tomorrow and I will tell you more about my Edouard and my Joseph.

EIGHT

The next morning Isabelle was in the dining room when I came in for breakfast. She was wearing a sleeveless African print blouse, which I guessed she had had made here or on another trip to Africa, and a string of beads which also looked to be from here. She heard me greet the guesthouse staff.

'That's not Swahili, is it?'

'No, that's the local language. One of about ten words I know. I love the way they say good morning. It means "I am glad you survived the night without being killed."'

'Is that because of the conflict?'

'No, it's historical. Long before the conflict, and long before the Europeans were here. The risk was being killed by animals in the night.'

'Makes our words seem a bit boring,' she said.

'May I join you?' I asked.

'Yes, of course.'

Her laptop was open and I saw a picture on her desktop.

'Is that your family?'

'Yes, all five of us.'

Open on her screen was a picture of three girls in the foreground and the parents just behind them on one side; two of the girls looked very similar, pale eyes and light hair; the other sister had dark hair and dark eyes. The man, who looked to be about sixty, had a full head of dark hair and was looking fondly at Isabelle's mother.

'Your parents look happy. Like a couple in love.'

'I think they are.'

She looked at the picture for a moment and then back at me. I think she could tell that I wanted to know more.

'My father was a young, Swiss diplomat posted to Santiago at the beginning of the Pinochet regime. He wasn't very high in the chain of command and Switzerland was fairly anti-Communist in those days, but he apparently was able to help some people.

'My mother is a dancer and choreographer. Comes from an artistic family. My father was engaged to a woman in Switzerland when he was posted to Chile.

But he saw my mother at a performance in Santiago, and was so moved by it that he looked her up afterwards. He invited her to give a recital at the embassy so he'd have a reason to see her.

'They started seeing each other. They said it was just going out for a coffee at first. But then it became more intense. At the same time, my mother's company worked on a piece that was considered a protest against the regime. They used a song with a refrain from Victor Jara, you know, the protest singer, and the dance was considered an act of subversion.

'They never really told us how much risk she was in, but he arranged for her to perform at an event in Switzerland so he could get her out of the country. The Swiss weren't giving asylum to Chileans then, so he helped get her permission to stay for a few months in Switzerland on a cultural visa.

'And then he went there a little while later, broke off his engagement with his Swiss fiancée, and the next day asked my mother to marry him. She asked if he was doing it just so she could have citizenship and be safe. He said: "No, I'm doing it because I fell in love with you the first time I saw you dance."'

'That's quite a love story,' I said.

'Yes, a hard one to follow.'

'Meaning?'

'That's a hard ideal to live up to, or to find a man who lives up to that. To him.'

'And now? Are they … '

'I think they love each other deeply.'

I looked back at the computer screen and then at Isabelle.

'Do you go back to Chile often?' I asked.

'Yes, every few years. When we were growing up in Switzerland, we would spend part of our Christmas holiday there, which was summer in Chile. The two places have a lot in common. Mountains, skiing, order, obsession with order.'

She raised her eyebrows at this part.

'Have you been?' she asked.

'No, not to Chile. I spent a summer in Brazil and another in Peru when I was in university. I did some hiking in the Peruvian part of the Andes. And of course I bought copies of Neruda to try to seduce girls when I was in university.'

'Did it work?' she asked, smiling.

'Sometimes.'

'I'm glad my countryman could be of service.'

'Well, I must go. Third interview today,' I said.

She was looking at her computer screen as if she had work to get to.

'Oh, and uh, speaking of love stories,' I continued.

Isabelle's eyes widened.

'This is for you. It's a good one too. So far.'
I handed her a memory stick.
'It's in an audio file. The first two interviews.'

INTERVIEW 3 — MARY OF KIVU

When a man like Edouard is scorned, he can make trouble. Men have their pride.

With my Joseph away, I kept studying and studying. It was my escape.

And Edouard, he was always there. He would say: *Let's go for a walk. Let's go to a party. Meet me tonight beside the school.* Always that face, from the cold smile to the look of a small boy to that dangerous grin. And always in the back of my mind, I was wondering if those soldiers would come back and what they would do.

I so wanted Joseph to come home, even just for a visit. I knew, of course, that he could not. It was expensive and long, and his family was saving all their money to send him to university. I heard that Joseph was working on weekends and during breaks so he could make some money to help pay for school.

I wished for letters. I wished he would write me poems or send some news, anything. He sent postcards sometimes. They would arrive weeks later. And he would tell me nothing more than that he was doing well and studying hard and that he missed me.

I believed that he thought my parents would open the letters, that they would get them before I did.

For another year, this went on. Edouard brought presents to my mother: fish from the lake, fresh milk, once even a new wrapper for me. He told my mother what he knew about the rebels and that everything was safe. That they were far away from us. I saw him talking to my father. I asked my father what Edouard wanted.

'If your Joseph does not come back, this Edouard will give a good bride price for you,' my father said.

I looked to the ground and then looked him in the eye.

'Don't I get to decide which man I marry?' I said, nearly crying but holding back the tears.

'His parents say he is in line to marry first,' my father said. 'They will give him the land and a motorcycle and the bride price before Joseph. Joseph will have to work some time, make money to pay back what they have borrowed from the village to pay for his school. It is only fair. He is the one who got to go away for university.'

'Let Edouard find a girl who wants to marry him then,' I said and stormed off to my tree.

Sometime after that, Edouard came to where I was reading, but this time he came with a woman on his arm. I knew her. Her name was Olive. Everyone knew she was a girl who would go with sugar daddies. A snack and a lift in a car and she would do whatever a man wanted.

'Hello, little sister-in-law,' Edouard said, putting his arm around Olive in a way no respectable girl in the village would let a man do in public.

'Hello, Olive, hello, Edouard,' I said, and turned back to my book.

I heard them whispering but I could not hear what they were saying, and they walked on. Then I looked up and saw that Edouard was looking back at me. His look was a mixture of scorn and anger, and then his eyes turned sad.

In all this time, there was only one real letter from Joseph. I knew it was a long bus ride from Kampala to Kivu, and an expensive trip for someone from our village, and that the mail rarely made it across the borders.

I knew that Joseph had to save all the money he had for his studies. I heard through his mother that he was doing well, that he would be home in a year, that he would begin looking for work near Kivu.

The one letter he sent me came via Edouard. It talked only about the campus and the city of Kampala and his courses and the books he had read. It could have been from a friend or a brother. This was not the kind of letter that would come from a lover. I could not understand. I didn't know what it meant. Where were all those things we had dreamed of together? Did he think that Edouard or his mother was reading his letters?

Oh, but I imagined. Eh, don't young girls like to imagine?

I could see Joseph watching his classmates go to discos. Those discos where girls would throw themselves at men. I could imagine that when his friends did this, he would make the excuse that he didn't have enough money, that he needed to save all his money for his studies.

And then I could imagine a friend telling him: 'The girls don't cost that much, Joseph. A beer or two, a meal.' And in my mind these friends of Joseph laughed just like Edouard. I could imagine those girls in the shimmering outfits hanging around the *mzungus* and the sugar daddies in the bar. I imagined they dressed like Olive, only worse.

Even if he didn't go to those discos, I could imagine his classmates, all those girls, so smart and so pretty, much more sophisticated than me, the girl from the countryside.

I was sure that my Joseph would not have been able to resist.

And then, after all that time waiting, I heard from his mother that he was coming home. She didn't tell me anything else—if he was engaged to someone else, if he had a job in Goma, nothing. She knew only the day he left, not even when he would arrive.

The arrival times for these buses are unknown. They have to wait at borders. They break down. The road may be closed for a few days where it has caved in. I would have been there waiting at the bus stop, but I had no idea what time he would arrive.

And then a neighbor said she heard the bus had arrived.

You can imagine how my heart was beating. I reread the poems he gave to me. I imagined what I would say to him. I could not think about anything else except when I would see him again. I imagined that he was catching up with this family, telling them all that had happened, and that he would soon be coming to visit me. I would wait under the tree. He would know to find me there. He would know I would be there reading like I always was. Waiting for him.

I wondered at times if it could be true. He must have become engaged to another girl or fallen in love with another girl. I could not bear it.

Still he did not come. I tried to read. I tried to calm myself that he had things to do. He was now a university graduate and he had things to tend to. Maybe he already had a job. He would soon come.

But he did not.

It was approaching the end of the day, a whole day after he had returned, and I could bear it no longer. In my culture, a girl is not allowed to pursue a boy, to go to his house and call on him. That is for girls like Olive, girls who never get married.

Girls who don't bring a good bride price.

But I did not care. Let his family think of me what they would.

Let my father be angry at me and tell me I was a dishonor. Let the village talk about me. I picked up my books and put them in my bag and I walked to his house.

My dress had been well-pressed at the beginning of the day but by then it was covered with dust from sitting on the ground and was wrinkled. I did not care. I needed to see him. I needed to know if he had waited for me.

I walked to his house. He must have seen me coming. He walked to the edge of the yard. There he was, with a face like a man now. I was imagining his arms around me. I wanted them around me. Then I saw the look on his face. It was cold and angry and sad all at the same time. Before I could say anything, he spoke.

'I have nothing to say to you.'

'What is it, Joseph, my love? I waited so long … '

'My brother told me what happened.'

'Joseph, nothing happened. He invited me to a wedding party. That was more than two years ago. I danced with him. The rebels came through and I ran home. Nothing happened.'

'That's not what he said.'

'Joseph, I have nothing to hide. I did nothing I should regret.'

'Go away. I want nothing to do with you. If you want to marry him, do as you wish. You have every right to marry whomever you want. You can throw yourself on any man you please.'

Then he turned and walked back into his house and left me standing there.

I wanted to die.

[Mary stopped and looked away and then started again.]

Have you ever had the feeling, Mr. Masterson, of having your heart ripped out? When I first read the romantic poets, I thought it was just a figure of speech.

But as I stood there in his yard, I knew that it was real. It was the physical feeling of having it ripped out. The pain was as real as any sickness. Three years imagining the moment when my Joseph would come back. Three years of imagining what it would feel like to feel his eyes on me against, to hear his voice, to anticipate all that would come. And then this.

I suppose I deserved it. I suppose Edouard could have told him the truth or what he thought was the truth, that if not for those soldiers, I might have been with him. But I hadn't.

Tell me, Mr. Masterson. Does it matter, do you suppose? What if I had?

What if, on a night of dancing and watching other couples, what if I had wanted his brother? And what if Joseph had been with a girl at one of those discos? Would his love for me be any less? Would mine for him?

The priest doesn't like us to talk like this, does he? The men around here, they cannot accept that talk from women, eh. But would it have mattered? If Joseph knew what I felt for him and he for me and we wanted to be together, would God make me drown in my own tears or in my own pee or in my own blood that came every month?

I could swear that I saw Edouard looking at me from inside the house, or maybe I wanted him to see this. Maybe I wanted him to look at me so I could look back at him with all the anger I could command. Or maybe I wanted to see if he was brave enough to come out and tell everyone that he was in love with me, if he really was. I just wanted to see him show his face so I could tell him and everyone that I loved Joseph and that no one could take that away.

You know, Mr. Masterson, my father raised me to be proud. I

don't know if that is a curse or a blessing.

As I stared at my Joseph, I held my head high. I did not fall to the ground like one of those little girls, like my sisters might have, or like those girls in those silly stories from nineteenth century Europe that they made us read before I made the headmistress give me real books. Before Joseph gave me real books.

Joseph turned and went into his house. He said nothing more to me. I would not beg.

I began walking. I did not know where I would go. I did not want to go back to my tree. I did not want to go back to my house. I did not want to go back to the school where I had spent all those years with other girls. The school where I would soon have a teaching certificate. I would have walked to the lake and rowed myself out to an island just to sit and think. But that would only make me think of Joseph.

So I just walked. I left the road and walked on the trails that went further away from our village. I did not want to see people I knew. I did not want to see anyone. I did what they always told us *not* to do. I walked alone into the hills past the waterfall, up along the river.

You should see the place, Mr. Masterson. Maybe you did when you drove here. There is the big waterfall you see from the main road. Then you can follow the river far away from the main road where there is a forest and only a few farms and few families. And then you walk up to a point where you can see down onto the clouds. You are looking down onto Lake Kivu from higher than the clouds.

I stopped along the way and sat down and wrote my Joseph a poem. Eh, the silly verses of a schoolgirl.

Why would I hide my love,
You who have taught me to sing,
To sing and shout love,
To feel love in the words on a page,
To feel it in English and Swahili and all the languages poets
have ever used.
And in the places where words have no language,
Where feelings have no words.
Could you doubt that I would proclaim my love only for you?
And could you doubt that I would wait for you?
For my life has only been waiting until you came,
Moments that existed and passed to make the Me
Who has waited for You.
The urn, not of what Was
And is frozen in the moment of its wonder,
But the urn that was Waiting
For You to bring it to life.
The urn of what Is.

I struggled with the final line. I wrote five or six alternative verses for the ending. Some of them ended with the urn coming to life on its own. In one version it is my own finger that brings the urn to life. In another version the urn cracks, never to be brought to life. But I scratched out all those alternative final verses and left it like that: 'For you to bring it to life. The urn of what Is.'

I continued walking.

I knew my father and my mother would chastise me if I told them I came this far alone, that I was walking out there in the hills above the falls. But it was the only place I could be right then. If it was poetry that made my monthly blood come, it would be sadness that made me into a woman strong enough to stand on her own.

As I continued walking I was so lost in my thoughts that I forgot for a moment where I was.

My father is not like many of the other coffee farmers around us who think that the spirits of the dead inhabit these empty forests by the river above the falls, or that a magic spell can curse their crops. He believes those things when he wants to. But he is not afraid of them. He has a secondary education and he reads and he knows things and he wanted the same for us.

You see, Mr. Masterson, I was not supposed to be here in these hills because this is where the rebels sometimes come to hide.

Those women in the hospital, all those women they are trying to fix. Those women who look at you with the blank stares. Those women who have no home to go back to because their husbands and their families have kicked them out. They know. They can tell you. They can tell you about the moment. They remember exactly where they were when they heard those men coming. You never forget that moment. You may forget the rest. You may try to forget the rest. You may have to forget to survive. But you remember when you first heard those men coming.

[A child cried just then and Mary looked away from me and toward the door. This next part she said in English.]

Mr. Masterson, you come back tomorrow and I will tell you what happened.

[She turned back to me just as she was standing up to leave the room and spoke again.]

To care for a child, Mr. Masterson. It's magical what that cry for help can do to you. I could not imagine before. Maybe you know what I mean. To hear a voice that needs you and only you.

117

[Before I could ask anything more, she was flowing out the door. I sat in silence until one of her assistants called my name and escorted me outside.]

NINE

When I returned to the guesthouse that evening, the young woman on duty, Sandra, handed me my room key and told me there was another guest. Another *mzungu*.

'Many *mzungus* today,' she said.

I went straight to the dining room, where I found the man sitting and reading. He looked up as I entered. He was about my age, mid-thirties, dark, short hair, a fashionable beard of a couple days' growth, and was dressed in a polo shirt and jeans.

'Good evening,' he said.

'Hey,' I said, and began to sit down at the other table in the dining room.

Just then Isabelle came in.

'Hi,' she said, greeting me with a smile.

She had the memory stick in her hand and extended it to me.

'Thank you,' she said. 'It's … '

'I'll put the next ones on there for you,' I said.

'Thanks. Did you meet our fellow guest?'

'Hello, I'm Raul Saavedra. Good to meet you,' he said, standing up. Now I understood his slight Spanish accent.

'Keith Masterson,' I said, moving the short distance that separated us and extending my hand.

'Ah, yes, Father Ningonwe told me about you,' he said, shaking my hand.

'Oh. How do you know him? Are you also … '

I was trying to sound non-judgmental.

'I am also with the Church, yes, based in Rome.'

'Investigating the miracles?' I asked.

Now I could not stop the cynicism from creeping in.

'Well, it's not really an investigation. I'm the advance scout or something like that. It sounds like I am after the same story that you are. And Isabelle too, I think.'

'You're doing an investigation for the Congregation for the Doctrine of the Faith?' I said.

'Yes, that's us. But don't expect me to wear robes and gold chains. I'm about the level of an intern,' he said, offering a deferential smile.

He seemed to be used to this kind of skeptical reception from *mzungu*-journalists.

'Who reports to a head of state,' I said, a serious look on my face.

'I think there are at least six or seven levels of bureaucracy before I could even get to his appointment secretary. I see the Pope from his balcony at an occasional Mass. And once, walking down the hall to a meeting.'

Again, he gave a deferential smile. I wasn't sure if this was part of his presentation, his attempt to put us at ease, or if he really was just an intern and genuinely self-deprecating.

'Shall we sit at one table?' Isabelle said.

'Yes, of course, will you join us, Father … Saavedra?' I said, even though I really didn't want him to.

'Just Raul, please. I'm not a priest,' he said, again using his boyish grin.

'Ah.'

We all sat down at the table.

'I studied for the priesthood and then took time off to do a master's degree before I took my vows. I wanted time to think about it and I wanted to study more, and the Church obliged me. Now I'm working on my doctorate. They don't seem to be in a hurry with me.'

'I see,' I said.

There was silence among the three of us.

'I heard that Mary is talking to you,' he said, his Spanish accent coming out as he said this.

'Yes she is. You have your sources. Even though you've just arrived.'

I looked at Isabelle.

'Don't worry, I won't ask you to tell me what she said. I was just making conversation. It's not a big village and there are no other journalists that Mary is talking to. I am sure more are coming, though.'

His English was nearly flawless—slow and studied, his accent coming out only occasionally.

'We've just barely started,' I said.

'You know what happened to her?' Raul asked.

'You mean … '

'During the conflict,' he said.

'No, we haven't talked about that yet. But I've heard about it,' I said.

'I'm sure she'll tell you her version soon enough,' he said.

I could feel Isabelle's eyes on me.

'And will you send it out to the world, for everyone to read?' Raul asked, and seemed to look at both Isabelle and me when he said this.

'I have to figure out what I'm sending out first,' I said.

'But you will. All these things she's telling you. Her story? Her life?' he continued.

Isabelle's gaze became more intense.

'She must be telling me for some reason. I am assuming she wants her story told.'

'Yes, I suppose,' he said, and looked away from me and toward Isabelle. 'There are always reasons for telling stories.'

'You know what happens after women here are raped, don't you?' Isabelle said, looking at Raul. 'How they're rejected?'

It was the first time I had heard her take on that activist, NGO tone.

'Yes, I do,' he said.

'It's important to get this out,' she said.

She was convincing when she used this tone.

Sandra brought out our food and we all turned to our plates for a moment.

'So, what is your dissertation about?' I asked.

Raul smiled an embarrassed smile.

'Is it that kind of topic?' I asked. 'Or is that what everyone asks you.'

'A little of both. You know, I think my topic must seem a bit useless perhaps, at the very least obscure compared with, say, the priest in the church in the village I grew up in, or to my father, who is a farmer.'

'Farm boy to scholar?' I said.

'Of course. Anything to get out of working on the family farm.'

'Not interested in becoming a gentleman farmer?'

'Picking olives and raising sheep to make cheese did not

seem interesting to me. My family is not intellectual and they didn't see the importance of university, especially to study philosophy or theology. But I wanted to study. I knew that from the time I was very young. And I was good at learning languages. I wanted to be able to carry out conversations like the kind my village priest had. The Church was … '

I smiled.

'Is it funny?' he said.

'No, I just never would have imagined a village priest as an intellectual.'

'You need to come to my village. In a small town in Spain where everyone is a farmer and just has secondary education, priests are sometimes the most educated ones.'

I nodded.

'I'm studying the history of religion, of Christianity. I'm focusing on encounters between the official Catholic Church and other religions during the time of Spanish colonial expansion.'

I shook my head.

'I'm interested in the first contacts between the Catholic Church and other cultures, or civilizations, and their religions.'

'So what's your argument?' Isabelle said.

I noticed the softness in her eyes as she looked at him. I had seen the green in them shine like this before.

'I'm particularly interested in an encounter that took place between the Church and Mexica or Aztec leaders in the early 1600s. I'm reading through the archives of the West Indies in Sevilla and in the Vatican about the encounter.

'Their debates about God, their cosmology, and then tracing how the Catholic Church in Mexico took on a different style than in Europe. In Brazil, they call it *sincretismo*.

'I'm reading about an encounter between some of the Vatican's best minds and some of the most learned priests among the indigenous Mexicans. It would have had translation between Spanish and Nahuatl, which was the Swahili of its day in Mexico. Catholic leaders argued the superiority of their religion to the Mexica, who refused to give in and who explain their beliefs, two societies with extremely well-developed views of the world, each convinced of the righteousness of its own. The Mexica or Aztecs were defeated already, of course, except for a relatively weak resistance. But it may have been one of a few times when the Catholic leaders were not destroying their codices and burning men at the stake if they found indigenous relics in their homes.

'The Church wants to believe that a certain Catholic purity prevails, that the encounters always evangelize the other. They speak about those moments of meeting new believers in a kind of romantic way.'

He stopped for a moment and looked at both of us, watching, I think, for signs that we were following his line of reasoning.

'So, what's your take on those encounters?' Isabelle asked.

'There are many examples of how the Catholic Church has been influenced by those encounters, by *all* encounters with the different, non-Judeo-Christian-Muslim religions.'

'That's not nearly as ridiculous as some doctoral dissertations I heard about in graduate school. And seems the Vatican is interested in the topic,' I interjected.

I turned to my food for a moment and looked to Isabelle.

'How did that get you to Lake Kivu?' she asked.

'I'm not sure. Luck, I think. I was having a coffee with one of the staff in the office that investigates miracles and he was try-ing to figure out who they would send here, to find out more about Mary of Kivu.'

He looked at us both for a moment as if he wanted to know if he could trust us.

'They wanted to send someone who was not obviously a priest, and not clearly from the Vatican. Someone who wouldn't insist on five-star accommodation. Someone who spoke French.'

Raul stopped.

'Should I be telling you all this?' he asked, looking in my direction and then giving a warmer look to Isabelle.

'Why not?' I said. I could not keep my voice from sounding defensive.

'I read your book on the Lord's Resistance Army. You use most everything that comes your way. I imagine many people did not expect to see all those things they said end up in your book. Or to hear your views about them in such, well, a criti-cal way.'

Critical was said with the long 'i's of Spanish.

Isabelle looked at me as well; this time the look was not soft.

'So, are you using *this*?' Raul said, in a voice that did not give away if he was serious.

'Right now I'm having dinner,' I said and smiled.

* * *

I had trouble sleeping again. There were voices swimming in my head. I had heard stories firsthand from *genocidaires* and other killers who did not repent in even the smallest ways as they recounted their deeds. And there were my father's sto-ries and those pictures he took from war zones. And there was imagining him losing his voice, imagining what he might be going through as his esophagus was being eaten away by can-cer.

But there were other voices that I heard, louder voices. Voices of small children—girls, running and playing—some speaking English, some speaking Swahili, some Bosnian. The loudest of all was the bright-eyed little girl who pulled her hand away from me when I thought she was reaching out to me.

TEN

The next day, I was ready just after my usual time of 8:00 AM. My driver was waiting. When we arrived at Mary's house, the crowd had already formed. Many people had obviously spent the night there. But they were not all waiting in line as they usually did. Most were talking amongst themselves and standing around the perimeter of Mary's house, looking toward it.

'What do you think's happening?' I asked.

'I will go ask,' my driver said.

He came back a few minutes later.

'One of the staff at Mary's house, a houseboy who works in the garden, he tried to kill himself. Mary saved him. He had set fire to the small house he stays in. She walked in and saved him. They say the flames engulfed her but she came out unharmed. And she brought the house boy with her.'

'Why did he try to kill himself?' I asked.

'They are saying that he was a rebel and that he was made to kill his own family and that he couldn't live with the memory.'

I heard women singing and ululating, as I had a few days before.

'Now they are singing that Mary has saved another.'

As we listened to the women sing, several pickup trucks pulled up. There were four or five young men in the back of each. They were wearing the clothes of civilian villagers, but they looked serious. I could not see if they had weapons.

'We should go, Mr. Keith.'

'Who are those men?'

'I don't know. The elections are coming and things are tense. Not everyone around here would save a former rebel. It's better if we leave.'

'This is more than the elections, isn't it?' I said. 'Wait a minute while I go and talk to the women in the tent.'

My driver continued to look tense, which I didn't like because we had been in situations I thought were far worse, and he was usually calm even when I was apprehensive.

I looked him in the eye and then stepped out of the jeep. I walked to the reception tent and asked the woman on duty what was happening.

'There are people who do not want Mary to tell her story. She will not talk to you today.'

I nodded. 'Of course. Can I help in some way?'

'You will help if you stay away right now. It is better if she is not seen with a *mzungu* journalist.'

She looked at my jeep, which had 'press' stenciled on it.

Then I saw another two pickup trucks arrive. Several more men got out. This was definitely more than the elections.

Normally I would not have left; these were the moments I gathered the most interesting information and observed the things that usually reached the international media only via secondhand reporting. But now, as I looked back at the tent, I saw that the woman who had received me was looking at me with an urgent expectation that I should leave. I did not, today, want to be part of the problem.

I returned to my jeep and nodded to my driver for us to leave.

* * *

'You didn't get an interview today?' Isabelle said, when I was back at the guesthouse before lunchtime.

'No, and you didn't go to the office either, I'm guessing.'

Her tone was lighthearted, as if school had been canceled for the day; mine was tense.

'I went, but when I got there they told me that, with the threat of election violence, I should either stay in the guest house or go see the gorillas or go to Kigali,' she said.

'There is definitely something up, but it's more than just the elections.'

'Have you been to see the gorillas?' she asked.

I looked back at her as if this was the least of my worries or interests at the moment.

'Um, yes, on the other side of the volcanoes, on the Rwandan side, but I only got a glimpse of them. There are supposed to be more of them on this side,' I said.

I was feeling impatient and reading messages off my mobile phone.

'Should we go?' she asked.

I turned and looked at her. I was texting a colonel in the Congolese armed forces who had given me his number and told me I could call or text him anytime I needed. He turned out to be as simple and honest as he had seemed when I met him.

'Sure. Yes,' I said, distracted. 'I suppose there may be no option.'

'You can't finish the story with Mary for the moment. And my office authorized my car and driver for me to go to the national park, so we can take my jeep if you want.'

I looked up from my phone, not sure what this invitation meant, if anything, and much more concerned about staying connected to Internet for the next days and finding out what was happening. I got a message back from the colonel that it should be safe in the national park but that there were reports of movement by rebel troops.

'Okay,' I said. 'But let's take my jeep and driver. He's got experience in tough situations. Plus your driver is a Rwandan Tutsi. It's safer for him to leave Congo or to stay put for the moment.'

Isabelle gave me a puzzled look.

'People are saying the violence is threatening to pick up again between the Congolese Tutsi rebel groups that the Rwandan government supports and the former Rwandan *genocidaires*. The Congolese army is more likely to support the former *genocidaires*. It's not so safe to be Tutsi in this part of Congo at the moment.'

* * *

'So, have you been to see the gorillas?' Isabelle asked my driver once we were in my jeep and on our way.

'Me, no,' he laughed. 'That is for *mzungus*.'

'Why?' she asked.

'We live with them for centuries.'

'Well it's not like you see them in your villages,' she said.

'Pay five hundred US dollars for that? Eh? Even though it is less for us than you *mzungus*, we don't do that. Pay to see gorillas picking fleas off each other and sniffing each other and beating their chest? My wife, and my mother and my sisters, would ask me why I didn't buy them new dresses instead.'

My driver made eye contact with me through the rearview mirror, giving the slightest smile.

* * *

We had been driving for about three hours, sometimes talking, more often silent, occasionally dozing off. Just before the sun began to set and we had about an hour remaining to reach our lodge, I leaned forward and met my driver's eyes in the rearview mirror.

'Do you see that?' I asked him.

'That is not normal,' he said.

'What?' Isabelle said.

'We're already in a controlled area, it's part of the national park, and if there are fires, either houses are being burned down or the villagers are being allowed to cut trees and make charcoal, which is prohibited in the conservation areas next to the park,' I said.

My driver slowed and we could make out a military vehicle and a group of five or six women on the side of the road.

I nodded at my driver and we stopped. There were two soldiers, both of whom looked to be twenty at the most. The women were wearing African wax print dresses in yellows and blues, some with sweaters on, some with headdresses. They were holding their arms up and speaking rapidly. They looked anguished.

The two soldiers had their guns pointed to the ground. Their expressions were blank.

My driver and I stepped out and Isabelle followed. I looked

back at her protectively. She hesitated for a moment when she saw my look and then came up behind us. The evening air was beginning to cool, and smelled smoky.

My driver translated for us.

'What happened?' Isabelle asked.

'She was raped ... rebels ... ' he said.

Isabelle looked as if she wanted to step forward and reach out to the women. We did not need to ask which of the women it was. One had a headwrap that covered much of her face, and she was crying and shaking and occasionally wiping her eyes with the ends of her headwrap.

'And they took her daughter away and killed her son,' my driver said, continuing to translate.

I introduced myself in Swahili to the two soldiers, who looked at me with indifference but no menace. I asked if we could take the woman anywhere for help and they said they would take her to the clinic nearby. I motioned in the direction of the park and one of them nodded.

'What will they do?' Isabelle asked.

'They'll take her to the health post inside the park.'

'Shouldn't we take her back to Goma or ...?' Isabelle started to ask.

'No, it's better inside the park. She'll be safer.'

Isabelle just looked at me. I remembered as I saw the distress on her face that this was her first time in Congo.

'The rebels don't come in here. It's a protected area, meaning there are more government soldiers. I offered for us to take her to the clinic but they said they will. Listen, can you call someone from your organization? Maybe they can send someone to meet them at the clinic, someone from here, if not tonight, then first thing tomorrow, make sure she gets the help she needs. It couldn't hurt. And then we'll know what happens too.'

Isabelle nodded. I could tell that she was having difficulty staying focused. She kept looking at the woman, and then back at me. She went back to the jeep and got her mobile phone and made some phone calls. She nodded at me a few moments later.

'Yes, yes. I'm sorry,' she said, trying to control tears and, I suspect, fear. 'I just … I've never dealt with this, I mean directly, like this, you know.'

Her accent was coming out the more distressed she became. She made another phone call and passed her phone to my driver. He passed it back to her after explaining to the person on the other end where the clinic was and where we were.

Isabelle stood by the side of the road with her phone in her hand, just holding it out in front of her and looking at me and then at the woman. Her look suggested that she was finally beginning to grasp all that the green hills and volcanoes were hiding.

'Should we go with them?' she asked, coming back toward me.

'We can if you want, but I don't think there is much more we can do. We can trust these soldiers, and I just called a colonel I know. He said he will make sure she gets to the clinic safely.'

I was interrupted by the woman's crying. She was louder this time, and rocking with uncontrollable and inconsolable sadness. I could hear her repeating a word: *binti*, daughter. We all knew what it meant when the rebels took young girls.

I nodded at the soldiers.

'Can't we do anything more?' Isabelle asked me.

'They're doing what they should be. Taking the woman to the health post, making sure she is safe, getting the medical care she needs. She has women from her village with her. A local woman from your organization will meet her at the health post. Sometimes the best we can do is stay out of the way.'

'I feel like I want to reach out to her, to ... '

'Yes, I know. So do I. But would that be for *you*, because you need it, or because you think she needs you to do that?'

My tone was softer than my words suggested.

She did not respond.

We were silent the rest of the journey to our lodge inside the park. The relaxed quiet in the car had turned to a strained and worried silence; all three of us kept our gaze focused outside the windows.

It was dark by the time we arrived at the lodge. As we stepped out of the car, we knew there were massive volcanoes surrounding us, but in the night sky we could only imagine their location by where the line of stars ended. It was cooler here at the higher elevation, cool enough to need a jacket. My legs and body felt heavy from the drive and from what we had seen.

I found myself sighing. It might be starting up again. There might be many more women like these by the side of the road, fleeing their homes.

'Are you okay?' I asked Isabelle.

She was bending over slightly and I wondered if she was nauseous from what we had seen.

'Yes, ... just ... it's all just so fragile and there is so little we can do.'

I could sense that she was on the verge of tears.

'I feel that way pretty much every day I am here,' I said.

Without speaking, she moved slightly in my direction and I understood that she wanted me to embrace her. Her chin came to the height of my collarbone. Her hair was soft as it brushed my cheek; she had a distinct smell, like a light perfume that was fading as the day passed.

'Shall we drop our things in our rooms and then have dinner?' I asked, as she pulled away.

She nodded.

We checked into our rooms and met in the dining room a few minutes later. It was a large round dining area, with tree trunks serving as the supports (or giving the illusion of being the supports) and a high thatched ceiling, making it look like an enormous African hut. The windows went from the ceiling to about halfway down the walls. The lighting consisted of wall lamps that used thin woven branches as lampshades. There were two other *mzungu* couples dining when we entered.

Isabelle was wearing a black sweater now. Her face was slightly flushed, as if she had just splashed cold water on it.

'Where do you put all of this in your head?' she asked, after we were seated and had ordered.

'I write. And I make myself think about other stories, the few that have good endings. Happy ones, when that's possible. There are a few.'

'Tell me one,' she said.

'Let me see if I can remember one.'

I paused and enjoyed the expectant look on her face.

'Okay, this one may not sound exactly happy but, um, it's how it ends that is. Anyway, a few years ago I met a man in

Kigali, a Rwandan, mid-twenties. He worked as my guide on an article. He spoke French, Kinyarwanda, Swahili, English. Along the way, while I was interviewing genocide survivors, he told me that he too was a survivor.

'We were in a church where Tutsi families had been massacred. Then all of a sudden he said to me: "I know why the families came in here and what it was like. It was the same with my family. We thought it would be safe. Who could harm you in a church? My father had lived through some of the small genocides, the attacks on Tutsis, years before. Back then, when they went into the church, he told us, the Hutus did not attack them. But this time, they killed us in here."

'He said they began shooting, cutting them down with *pangas*, then they threw in a grenade. There was screaming and crying. It was true panic, but they were shocked that the Hutus would do this. He said they didn't believe the Hutus would do this in a church. Whatever you may say about the tensions between Hutu and Tutsi, they all go to the same churches and believe in the same God.

'He was eight years old when this happened. In the confusion, he called out to his mother and father. Then he realized there were many mothers and fathers and he had to call their names—something he had never done. So he called out his mother's name and his father's name. At first there was no answer. Then he called again and again. Finally his mother answered.

'She was dying. She knew she was dying. She told him to be strong. To know that she loved him. And that he would have to make it on his own but that she would always be with him and that he would find other people who would love him. That he would find another mother. Then she told him to pretend that he was dead.

'He hid under the bodies until the Hutu *genocidaires* left, and a few days later when the Rwandan Patriotic Front troops came in, he was among the few who had survived. Then a few months later, in his village, they chose substitute parents for the orphaned Tutsi children. The Hutus who remained and who did not participate in the genocide were part of helping the Tutsi children who survived.'

Isabelle's eyes seemed wide open again.

'There was a woman at the meeting who had the same name as his mother. He chose her as his new mother and she accepted him. He told her: "I won't call you Mother. I will call you by your name because then I will remember my first mother. Every time I call your name, I will honor her too." She told him she would be honored to be his mother's namesake.'

Isabelle nodded silently. She pulled the sleeves of her sweater so she was holding the ends in both of her hands, which together with her still slightly reddened eyes made her look like a younger version of herself. She wiped her eyes and sat up and took off her sweater.

'My mother told us stories of friends who were caught up in the political repression in Chile. One family fled to Brazil, thinking it would be safer there, and then had to flee the Brazilian repression. Next they went to Panama, which also had a coup that overthrew a leftist government. Then they finally went to Europe.

'For years, the family kept copies of their documents and a small suitcase in the closet by their front door, ready to leave at a moment's notice. Whenever they moved, one of them would be responsible for carrying the suitcase. Once, when we visited their house, I remembered what my mother had told me. So when everyone was in the other room, I went to the front closet and saw a small suitcase. They lived in Geneva like we did. I must have been twelve or thirteen.

'One of the children, who is my age and has her own family now, does the same. She has copies of documents and a few photos in a small escape suitcase in the closet by the front door of her house.'

She paused and looked out the window into the night sky.

'I suppose other people talk about their favorite bands, concerts, things like that,' I said. 'We could try that.'

She looked back at me. We smiled about the same time and our eyes stayed on each other longer than before. Her smile looked to me to be that of a woman or a girl who was six or fifteen or fifty or the lovely thirty-something she was now.

* * *

We started the next morning a little after six. Isabelle was able to call her staff and find out that the woman had made it safely to the clinic. This lifted our mood enough to allow us to focus on the adventure of the day.

The morning air was still and clear. We both wore hiking pants and sweaters. My driver took us to the national park headquarters, where we found our group, which included the two of us plus six other tourists and our guide. Our guide's name was Francois; he introduced himself in French and asked if all of us could speak French or if any preferred English. He wore a green uniform that could have belonged to a soldier or a park ranger. He was chewing on a long strain of grass, explaining how he approached the gorillas by mimicking them, and telling us how they spent their days: eating, grooming, sleeping, and making baby gorillas.

He smiled shyly as he said this last part.

He explained that we should stay at least ten meters away from them. This was not for our physical safety; they very rarely attacked humans. It was so we would not pass any diseases to them. In this encounter between primates, we are the dangerous ones. He told us that our group had a baby gorilla, just about two weeks old. If we were lucky, we would see it. But we were to keep our distance.

François did not respond at first to a question from another hiker, a young woman with a strong English-accented French accent, about why he had a gun.

'Just to be safe,' he eventually said, but he did not look her in the eye.

As we began walking towards the vehicles that would take us the first part of the journey, I leaned over to Isabelle: 'Do you think she knows that she's in Congo?'

Isabelle looked at me with complicity; she was, after the night before, becoming a veteran.

We hiked for nearly three hours, with François constantly on his radio getting information from trackers on where our group of gorillas was. The vegetation was often dense underfoot and overhead. We walked long stretches with a limited view of the sky and then came to occasional clearings through which we could see volcanic mountains and watch the hazy-blue sky becoming slightly bluer as the sun rose.

'Okay, they are just up ahead. Stay close to me and keep your distance. If one of the smaller ones comes running up to you, do not touch it.'

We came around a cluster of trees and there they were: *our* gorillas. It is, of course, a cliché to say that they look like us. Their human-like gestures, their five-fingered hands, their grooming, their deeply set and languid, dark brown eyes, all incline us to transpose human qualities onto them.

Watching them interact with each other it is impossible not to attribute near-human intentionality to their actions. As one adolescent gorilla holds up a piece of tree in his hands and swirls it, I think I can almost hear him laugh. As another taps on the head of a peer with a thud that must have hurt but was meant to merely provoke, we can imagine that we are watching early slapstick comedy or human child play, frozen in evolutionary stasis.

We saw the imposing torso and head of the silverback, who nearly always kept his back to us, as if facing us meant that he would have to confront us and chase us away—that he would have to exert energy. Occasionally he made a short and violent run and the ground shook slightly under his weight. I watched our guide, who never seemed frightened by this display of force.

Isabelle touched my shoulder and pointed to the infant gorilla, who was sitting on his mother's chest, the mother lying on the grassy forest floor with a look of relaxation and contentment. I smiled at Isabelle as we both looked at the tiny features: the oversized eyes and the miniature face framed by black fur that shot up in perfectly spaced, tiny spikes.

For a time, we simply crouched and watched the gorillas around us. I took a few pictures, but mostly I registered with my eyes. A young male gorilla came right up to us, first rushing and then slowing down as he passed us and seemed to deliberately brush against us. François asked us to move back a short distance.

Then he pointed to the large nests the gorillas use to sleep in the trees overhead.

I thought of the gorillas as ancient cousins on the cusp of complex social interaction but who had remained behind in this simpler state. Other moments, as I considered their elaborate nests in the trees, the females grooming the males and the males occasionally responding with gestures I interpreted as affection, I wondered—as most human visitors do, I suppose—who took the right path. I imagined this was the standard discussion at dinner tables in the lodges at night. It was impossible, with all that was happening around us, not to think about this.

A couple of hours later, we walked back via a different trail, through a series of small farms. We saw longhorn cattle and women carrying firewood. As I looked at their simple houses and watched them balance the wood on their heads, I tried not to think about what my driver had said: that the money a *mzungu* spends to see the gorillas could buy lots of dresses.

'Do you think they know how much we pay for this?' Isabelle asked.

'They do. And they know why there are more troops protecting the gorillas than there are protecting them.'

ELEVEN

We were back at our lodge by mid-afternoon. Isabelle read on her balcony while I went for a run through a village nearby, running on mostly deserted roads that offered views of the volcanoes and mountains. I passed an occasional cluster of huts where children ran toward the road and waved at me and I smiled and waved back. My legs were tired after the hours of hiking, but I hoped the run would make me even more physically exhausted—enough so that I might actually sleep through a whole night.

Before we had left Mary's village to come here, Raul had told us that he would also be nearby staying at the Catholic Church's guesthouse inside the national park. He too was unable to continue his investigation for the moment. We had all agreed to meet for dinner at our lodge.

At dinner time, I walked from my room the short distance to Isabelle's. She was sitting on her balcony looking out at the darkening sky. She was wearing a long, simple, sleeveless dress made of brightly colored woven cotton that might have been bought at an African boutique. It clung to her in a way that drew my eyes. I am sure she could tell.

She looked rested, her face calm and thoughtful.

'I can't help but feel impotent about it all, about what happened. Our life goes on, we go visit the gorillas, and there she is,' she said.

'It's important that we're here to tell about it. That has a purpose. *That's* why we're here.'

'I'm supposed to be doing more than that. My organization is trying to make sure that it doesn't happen. And helping them rebuild their lives afterwards. But I wonder if all we can really do is watch it happen.'

I don't think she wanted a response.

Raul was in the dining room already, reading. He closed his book and stood up to greet us. I could see that Isabelle's dress had the same effect on him.

'How were the gorillas?' he asked.

'Magnificent,' Isabelle answered, her French accent coming out. 'To see them in the middle of all this, is … either I wanted to cry more or I suddenly felt hopeful. Maybe both.'

Raul smiled a knowing smile. I felt a moment of insecurity in his simple, soft charm.

'I have been visiting some of the villages, meeting the local priest. These villages in the park have been spared some of the violence so they seem to me, perhaps, more optimistic. They talk of a Congo that could work. Some of them, anyway.'

'What you reading?' I asked, looking toward the book he put down on the table.

'If I tell you, will you use it against me?' he asked, with his boyish grin.

'Depends on what it is,' I said.

'I've been reading about the various historical accounts of Mary of Nazareth.'

He paused and looked at us, as if gauging how we would react to this topic.

'You have to excuse me. I spend so much time reading these

143

things that I assume that other people are interested in them. Let us talk about something else.'

'No, please, tell us,' Isabelle said as we sat down.

'Yes, please,' I said.

'Okay, but first, shall we order some wine, or do you want a beer?' he said.

'Wine would be great,' Isabelle said.

I nodded.

We ordered and then he continued.

'You know, I was reading this book for my dissertation but, really, I think it has much to say about what is happening now in Congo. The book has a theory that Judaism became matrilineal after the Bar Kokhba rebellion, a Jewish revolt against the Romans around the time of Christ. There are accounts that many Jewish women were raped by Roman soldiers and the Jews became matrilineal to keep the children in the tribe. To survive. Others say Judaism was matrilineal long before that.'

He looked at us to see if we were paying attention.

'Keep in mind that Jewish laws back then were a bit like what they are in the Yemen or places like that today. Adultery was punishable by death by stoning. Women went about with veils. A woman who was raped could be accused of adultery.

'So then the author goes into the different theories about Mary, about what we know about her from historical accounts. I'm sure you've heard the version that Mary was victim of rape by a Roman soldier, or perhaps had a relationship of some kind with one. She could have been coerced or maybe it was consensual. In some accounts, he even has a name, Pantera. In some versions, Pantera is a derogatory nickname the Jews used for all Roman soldiers. It was a slur against Christians for any non-Christian or non-Messianic Jews to imply that the mother of Jesus had sex with a man before she was married. Raped or not, that would make Jesus a bastard child. And not only a bastard but one fathered by the occupying troops, whom both Christians and Jews despised.

'And that's what we still do today, isn't it? In Spanish, we say *hijo de puta*. Son of a whore. In English it's 'son of a bitch'—son of a female dog. A female dog who can be taken by any male dog who smells her in heat. That is still our favorite way to curse someone.

'And if Mary were raped by a Roman soldier, or even if she had consensual sex with a Roman soldier, the story becomes really interesting. Joseph either took a woman who was not a virgin as his bride, or who was a victim of rape. In either case, a woman like that back then was generally stoned or sold into slavery, or she became a prostitute, if she wasn't one already.'

'We call them sex workers where I work,' Isabelle said.

'Of course we do. We've rehabilitated them, tried to give them back their humanity. Their rights. Back then, though, they were the lowest of all women, women with no reputation. And back then a woman's reputation was all she had. There are repeated instances in the Bible and the Torah and the Koran of women going to the well or the market, places in Middle Eastern villages where they were outside male relatives' control, where harm could come to them, where they were not being watched by a family member. A comment about their virtue could come from anyone. Once accused, there is almost no way you can prove your innocence. And in those times, what man would marry a woman with a question about her reputation?'

His eyes were intense. Then he was silent for a moment, as if giving us time to think about this.

'Think about it this way. It would be ridiculous, of course. I mean it would be impossible to create a global religion out of a story of rape, right? Okay, I know that. But I think sometimes that if Mary were a rape victim and Jesus the child of this rape, wouldn't that be reason for a religion? Wouldn't that be the most glorious form of empowerment of women, of embracing women, of humanity, and, in that case, wouldn't Joseph be a model for what we expect from men? Empowering, accepting, supporting—a man who stood up against an unfair patriarchal culture.'

He paused.

'That idea would probably not go over well with your employer,' Isabelle said.

'Sounds dangerously close to humanism. Not to mention feminism,' I said.

'Please, we're not all simpleton priests, blindly following what they tell us. We have a doctrine we're supposed to follow, and there are eras when doctrines become more conservative. But we're allowed to think and critique. It doesn't mean they will put that alternative point of view on the Vatican website.'

'No, I suppose not,' I said. 'But I think we will truly advance in women's rights when we don't need either a supreme being or a hero to save them. We will have laws that work and protection and rights ... '

'Probably,' he said, cutting me off. 'But in the real world, I'll take a very human story. One that we can relate to in our own flesh and blood.'

Isabelle's eyes were intense and weary at the same time, and I was sure she was looking at Raul in a new way.

146

* * *

Dinner was served slowly, one course at a time. It was not the multi-course fare of a fine French restaurant but, rather, the rhythm of rural Congo. We finished our first bottle of barely passable wine and ordered a second. We moved on to lighter topics, books we liked, places we had traveled.

'So, Raul, do you follow the celibacy part of being in the seminary?' I asked, emboldened by the wine.

He smiled slightly at my impertinence.

'That causes so much intrigue, doesn't it? A man or a woman who would decide not to have sex. For non-Catholics, and for Catholics, that is such a big question.'

'Well, yeah. It's a big deal. To swear off sex and all that comes with it.'

'No, I'm not. I have not taken vows. Before I entered the seminary, and since, I've had regular … girlfriends.'

He paused for a moment, drinking his wine. I wonder if he could tell that I was slightly annoyed with his response. I had the distinct feeling that this seminarian had a much more interesting sex life than mine.

'So, now I get to ask you: are you non-celibate?' he asked, the long Spanish 'i' coming out and making it seem like a lascivious word.

It wasn't clear if that question was directed to me or to both Isabelle and me.

'Yes, I am non-celibate,' I said. 'In general, anyway. At the moment, since I don't have a girlfriend, I'm temporarily celibate, I suppose.'

Raul held up his glass.

'To non-celibacy,' he said.

'Yes,' Isabelle said with just a slight shyness.

All three of us clinked glasses.

After the last glass of wine from our second bottle, Raul asked if we wanted more wine. I said I was ready to go to my room, hoping in my passive way, that Isabelle might say the same and that Raul would call his driver and head back to his lodge, and Isabelle would walk with me back to our rooms. Instead, they both said they would stay a little longer and wished me a good night.

As I left, I heard them switch into Spanish. I couldn't understand what they were saying, and I was not trying to understand, but the tone of their voices left me disconcerted. It seemed that a tension had been lifted after I left and that a light complicity replaced it. I slowed my stride as I walked away so I could hear their voices. I realized as I stepped out into the night air and walked back to my room that what bothered me most about this tone in their voices was precisely that it bothered me so much.

* * *

I could not sleep. The conversation reminded me that it had been a long time, excepting the few encounters with Lena, a Swedish aid worker I met in Kigali and occasionally went out with, since I had shared my bed.

To make myself sleep, to get myself to sleep, I let this memory come into my head. It was stored there, safe and kept away, as one of the best, one that needed to be guarded and held onto.

I met Sienna during graduate school. It was at a holiday party at a professor's house that she started a conversation and did that bounce with her hair and cocked her head in a way that on anyone else would have seemed silly. Later, she told me she came up to me because of the way I played with the professor's children.

'You don't try to make yourself the center of their attention. You have a way of going with their flow. Not many adults do that. Not many adults even *know* how to do that.'

I didn't really know what she meant or stop to think about it. I was looking at her eyes that were shining at me.

We hooked up the night we went to an R.E.M. show. I think it was our fourth or fifth time out together, but it was the first time at night, and the first time that involved wine. It was after the show and the campus was dark and quiet, and we walked with no defined destination. It was then that she told me that her sister had died just months before during childbirth. I thought Sienna was going to cry, but instead she turned to me and gave me one of those movie kisses. The R.E.M. songs in my head were the soundtrack accompanying her lips and her tongue on mine. I stopped to take a breath, and to look at her, and so that I could initiate the next kiss. I held her to me and moved my hands on her back and up the back of her neck.

'Come on,' she said, and grabbed my hand and dragged me in the direction of her apartment, which was just two blocks off campus.

As we approached her apartment building, we passed under a streetlight and I stopped her to embrace her from behind, and to bury my head in her hair for a moment. She had—still has, I imagine—intense red hair.

'Is your hair really this red?' I said, in a teasing voice. 'It's magnificent.'

'Of course it's real.'

'You never know. Anyone can have red hair,' I said in the same teasing voice.

'Well, there are some places you can't dye it.'

She had turned back to face me as she said this, reaching her hand up to my face and letting the back of her hand caress my cheek and then grabbed the back of my head. She laughed nervously.

'I think I've had a little wine. I think I'm about to be a little crazy,' she said. 'I think it's about time.'

She laced both arms behind my head and kissed me first on the lips and then on the neck and her body pressed against mine like it belonged there and should always be there, and she did so with a force and grace that made me think that I would do crazy things to be with her.

She pulled me, nearly running, into her apartment building. The elevator was moving slowly, so she grabbed by hand again and pulled me up the two flights of stairs, stopping at one bend of the stairs to kiss me again, letting her hand brush down the front of my pants in such a way that it was unclear if it was intentional.

She quickly opened and shut the door to her apartment and turned back to me without turning on any lights.

'My roommate's out of town,' she said.

She pulled me into her bedroom and sat me at the corner of her bed and then began to undress, only the lights from street-lamps providing a dim light.

'Now you can tell that it's really red,' she said.

She was teaching me then, showing me, with my hand and my mouth that she liked to come first and then climb atop me. And if she was teaching me this it was because, I guessed only later, she wanted to repeat this. She wanted me to be trained; she had plans for me. In the beginning, I gladly went along. Later it got out of control.

TWELVE

Isabelle knocked on the door of my room early the next morning; I could see as I opened the door that she was dressed for another day of hiking.

'Hey. Raul has offered to show us around some of the small villages where the Church has community development projects. Would you like to come along?'

'No, but thanks and please thank him for the invitation. I have some deadlines to meet. I'll be going into town later to get fast Internet. I'll probably be back late.'

'Okay. If you change your mind, text my mobile. I seem to have a signal most of the time.'

'Sure. Are you heading to breakfast now?'

'Yes. Raul is meeting me there.'

'Okay. I'll head over in a few minutes.'

She and Raul were still at breakfast when I arrived in the dining room. Raul smiled and rose to shake my hand.

'Isabelle says you're going into town later to use Internet,' Raul said. 'If you want to stay in town, we can have dinner at Coco Loco. Do you know it?'

I nodded. It was the restaurant and nightclub in the town closest to the gorilla park, a *mzungu* and Congolese hangout.

'Is it safe to be out late? With all that's going on, I mean,' Isabelle said.

'Yeah, the place is full of UN troops and aid workers. One

of the UN bases is not too far away. As long as our drivers are sober,' I said.

We agreed on a time.

* * *

It was about eight thirty in the evening when my driver pulled into the Coco Loco parking lot. It was packed with Land Cruisers, all of them white, most bearing logos of the UN, others with logos of international NGOs. The African drivers were congregated on one side of the lot, smoking and talking. I greeted them in Swahili and my driver walked over to join them.

There were several families dressed in tattered clothing at the entrance, extending their hands to beg. The guard at the entrance came over as they approached me and chastised them, holding his truncheon in the air with a lightness that insinuated a threat that none of us expected him to follow through on. The begging families retreated, but without true fear in their eyes, and returned to their resting places slightly farther from the entrance.

It was an open air building with zinc roofing covering most of it. There were simple tables and chairs, and a bar with a DJ station set up on one side. A menu board posted the day's offering in French and English. The waitstaff all wore bright red T-shirts with the logo and name of the place. This was still the pre-dance hour of the evening. More than half of the tables were filled, about two-thirds *mzungus* and the rest Congolese.

I quickly spotted Raul and Isabelle; she was wearing jeans and a sleeveless, tight-fitting blouse, not her usual international aid worker style. She stood up and gave me a kiss on both cheeks, and Raul stood to shake my hand. This time he put a hand on my shoulder as he greeted me.

'So, how were the villages?' I asked.

'Fascinating,' Isabelle said. 'There is a benefit to being within the park and having the protection of the military. Development can work when families are safe.'

She reached over and touched my arm.

'And I saw some children who were so adorable that I thought I would bring two for you.'

'Don't joke about that. They may take you seriously.'

'You're the one who is danger of that, I think. I've seen how children come up to you.'

'They see me as one of their own,' I said.

We ordered dinner and drinks and then more drinks, and around ten thirty the music started. The Congolese were the first to get up to dance. The music was a mix of African and Western. A few minutes after the music started, Isabelle saw some colleagues from her organization and, excusing herself, went to talk to them.

Raul and I turned our chairs so we could watch the dance floor. More Congolese and *mzungus* arrived.

The electricity went out and then came back when the generator was turned on, and the music resumed. A pleasant breeze wound its way through the space even as it began to get crowded.

'A little different than Rome,' I said, trying to make conversation.

'Yes. And yet, maybe exactly the same.'

He took a sip from his drink and then looked at me.

'You seem at home here,' Raul said. 'I take it you've been in this part of Africa for some time.'

'Yes, long enough that I'm confused about where home is.'

'But you can never really be from here, can you? I mean maybe unless you married an African or made a living working with Africans, not just us *mzungus*. Processing tea or coffee or something like that. I think if I were to have a parish here, I would have the same challenge. It would be difficult to ever be from here.'

'Do you *want* to become a priest and have a parish?'

He stared at me.

'You're not going to write this down, are you?'

'If I do, I'll change your name and all your details and make you come from a city in Poland and have you be much older. How's that?'

'That's good. To Raul, the old Polish priest,' he said, and held his glass up to clink with mine.

'So here's the story. I mean if you want to know what I think about the Church. I believe we can do good. I think that in places like this, we can do some good. Not just the spiritual part, which I think is good too, or can be. But in building or rebuilding community and creating connections between people. I also feel that we as the Church, as an institution, owe a lot to the communities for the harm we have done. You know the history. Our good must be made bigger than the harm we have done.'

I looked into his face; he was telling me this to the pulse of Congolese dance music. We both watched two tall *mzungus* talking to two young African women at the bar; we could see that some kind of negotiation was taking place.

'Certainly we can do as much good as any of the institutions that are here, no?' he continued.

'For sure,' I said, and then took another drink from my gin and tonic.

'That's not a very high standard, though. But what about the priest's life? You don't seem entirely suited for that.'

'No one is, huh? Then again, maybe none of us is suited to the married life and being monogamic,' he said, making one of his very few mistakes in English.

'Monogamous,' I corrected him.

'Yes, that's it. Are any of us set to be monogamous?'

'But that's different than being celibate,' I said. 'At least, it should be.'

'Yes, but even as priests or nuns, there are relationships, you know. You must be discrete and you might have to move when they tell you to and you have less control over being with someone you want to be with, but there are possibilities. You won't print that in your book, of course.'

He paused with a look of complicity, and then took another drink.

'What I mean is this. For anything or anyone we really care about, we have to give up some of our desires, right?'

He looked onto the dancing bodies.

'I mean, if you are married or you're with someone, you close certain doors, usually. So when an Isabelle comes along and you fall in love with her, you can't have everyone else beautiful and interesting who comes along. At least I don't think Isabelle would let you. Right?'

We both saw that Isabelle had finished her conversation with her colleagues and was walking towards us. She motioned

156

for us to join her on the dance floor. We obeyed.

Once on the dance floor, it seemed that the volume increased, or perhaps I stopped trying to filter it out and began paying more attention to the music. As I danced, I watched the African women and men whose use of their hips was professional compared to our amateur *mzungu* hopping. There was a seductive smell of perfumes and sweat flowing with the breeze. Isabelle held her arms in the air and twirled and made eye contact with Raul and then with me and I spun and everything merged into the beat: The African men and women and the *mzungus* and the begging families outside. The three of us moved simultaneously to accommodate the shifting bodies around us, and Raul and I moved into a synchronized orbit around Isabelle, one of us in front, the other behind and then trading places. She laughed and reached out her arms as if she might touch or caress us but never did.

One song flowed into the next and we were pleased that every time the music stopped it quickly resumed.

I only came back into a sense of time when I saw the young girls come in.

I had seen this before in *mzungu* bars here but never so many. They could have been eleven years old, certainly no older than fourteen; they were young African girls, dressed to look much older than they were, with low-cut blouses and mini-skirts and red and black leggings. They went up to the bar and not-so-subtly approached the *mzungu* men whose eyes they felt on them. Of course, there had been young women for hire in the bar all evening but none *this* young.

One of the staff at the bar began attempting to usher them out. This too was a dance, the girls largely ignoring the admonitions to leave and everyone knowing that they would not use force to remove the girls. Some of us watched; most continued dancing, apparently oblivious. Between the three of us, I seemed to be the only one paying attention to this. Moments later, the young girls got lost in the crowd or perhaps, finding no business, left.

The three of us took a break after the next song ended. Back at our table, I finished the last of my drink and said that I was ready to leave. The entrance of the young girls had left me disturbed. I invited Isabelle to go in my car if that was easier.

She looked at me and then at Raul.

'It's up to you, Raul. I would stay a little longer if you want to,' she said.

'Sure,' he said.

'I'll stay a bit more. We'll hike tomorrow,' she said to me, and then kissed me casually on each cheek, and then the two of them were on their way back to the dance floor.

I tried not to look back as I walked out, but of course I did. I took my time paying my bill and I could see them dancing and I swear I could see that Raul's hands moved to her back, just for a moment and then in the darkness of the dance floor, I am almost sure that his hands moved further down her body and that she moved into them. I am sure of it.

* * *

The next day was the last full day Isabelle and I had planned to stay at the park. We had left open the possibility that all three of us might hike together. I didn't see her at breakfast so I decided to work, then go for a run, then work more.

I still had notes to write up and an article to revise for Sam.

Isabelle texted me around noon saying she too had to work; she had a proposal to send to her boss in Geneva. She asked if I wanted to meet her and Raul for dinner later. I said I would see how far I got in my work, but that I might eat in my room and finish.

Okay, let me know, she texted back.

When the Internet at the lodge was out again, I decided to go back into town at the end of the day to send my revised article. It was already dark by the time I returned. From outside, I could see people in the dining room but I was in the mood to read and stay inside my head; and I was not interested in being a third wheel.

Coming to dinner? she texted when I was in the shower.

Just got back from town after sending e-mails. Exhausted. See you tomorrow am over breakfast? I replied.

OK, but we'll talk about you behind your back, she texted back.

I can take it, I texted.

I know you can, she replied.

* * *

After having dinner sent to my room, and finishing it, I took my laptop and went out on the balcony, where there were two wood-slat lounge chairs, and dozed off. The lightbulb on the balcony was burned out but the light from my laptop was enough to work by.

The cool air was just at the edge of tolerable with nothing but jeans and a sweatshirt. I looked up at the sky full of stars. The night was filled with the sound of insects, and birds and other animals I could only guess at; there was a darkness and density where the grounds of our lodge ended and the forest began. I felt protected, and at the very next moment I thought the forest might engulf the lodge and me with it, leaving no remains.

At first, I could not tell that it was her. I thought it was one of the several watchmen around us, the tall lanky men who wore black security guard uniforms and carried ancient rifles by their sides. As she got closer, and I realized it was Isabelle, I could see that she had on cotton drawstring trousers and a tank top and a wool blanket from her room wrapped around her shoulders. She was carrying a wine bottle and two glasses.

I felt a wave of anticipation, and at the same time I was slightly angry, if I had the right to use that word, about whatever was going on between Raul and her.

'Hey,' she said, 'I guessed you might still be awake. Can I interest you in some real wine?'

She turned the label towards me and I could see she was serious. Part of me was wondering about Raul, about what happened between them, if anything, and why she was now here, and part of me didn't care.

'How did you get that *here*?' I asked, rubbing my eyes.

'I got it in duty free in Paris on the way. I always have an emergency bottle of wine.'

'The stuff they serve here is pretty awful,' I said.

'Oh yes.'

'Have a seat. I'm not sure I'll last much longer before my eyes close for the night, but I'll try to be polite company,' I said.

She stepped over the balcony railing and I held her blanket and wine bottle and glasses as she did. She sat down in the lounge chair next to me and pulled her blanket over her legs. I opened the wine and poured two glasses. We clicked our glasses.

'To good wine when we most need it,' I said.

'*Santé*,' she said.

We both drank and looked at the stars, silent. I felt a rare sense of peace.

I had finished the chapter that had been challenging me. I was pleasantly, physically tired and thought I might be able to sleep a full night. And I had the unexpected pleasure of Isabelle's company, and was content just to float in the night-time noises and glance over occasionally at her. As I looked at her in the near darkness and could make out just a hint of her smell or whatever perfume she wore or soap she used, a smell that registered simply and pleasingly as *her*, I could imagine more, but I expected no more.

'So, are you involved with anyone at the moment?' she asked.

'No.'

'No one serious, or no one at all?'

'There's a woman I see every now and then in Kigali, a Swedish woman who works with an international aid agency, but nothing beyond the occasional ... '

'*Liaison*,' she said, finishing my sentence.

'Yes, *liaison*,' I said, imitating her French pronunciation of the word.

'When was your last serious relationship?'

It was a question that did not fit the moment.

'Excuse me?' I said.

'I'm asking about your past.'

'Do you really want to ... '

'This is the part where I'm trying to figure out if you're the relationship kind of guy.'

I was silent.

'See, here's what I'm thinking. I saw on your book jacket that you're thirty-four. I mean, you probably would have had a serious relationship by now.'

I took a deep breath and thought I could remain silent and that the question would go away.

'You don't want to talk about this, do you?' she said, with an air of disapproval, the 'i' in the *this* coming out like a Spanish or French long 'i'.

I turned my head toward her, realizing she was not letting go of this.

'Really, do you want to talk about that?' I said. 'Can't we talk about the stars or the gorillas or something else?'

I kept my voice calm; I controlled my infantile desire to ask what had happened between her and Raul.

'It had the potential to be such a nice bottle of wine,' I said.

'So you ask difficult questions, very personal questions, but you don't like them directed at you,' she said, affirming, not asking.

I sighed deeply and then ran my finger across my lips and took another drink of wine.

'I'm going to close my eyes and just imagine we could sit here and share a bottle of wine without having to go wherever you think you want to go with these questions.'

'You listen to Mary's story. You write down everything that comes your way in your books. I mean, really, your book on the Lord's Resistance Army is great.

'You are, how do you say, laser-focused on what you see and

honest about it all, and you go to every length to get the story. On the way here, we encounter a woman raped by the rebels. You tell intimate details of people in your books and you ask a seminarian about his sex life. And you want to sit and talk about the stars?'

'Yes,' I said, my eyes still closed, my voice sounding weary. 'Yes. Because I get stories like Mary's, and because my day job is to interview warlords and women raped by rebels, I would be very content just to talk about the stars and not to talk about why I don't have a girlfriend or whatever you think you want to know about me.

'Or simply not to talk,' I continued.

As if the next question had been poised in her mind even before I spoke, she barely paused.

'What moment would be on your Grecian urn?' she asked. 'You remember? When Mary cites the poem, 'Ode to a Grecian Urn'? Do you have a moment like that?'

I was silent, my eyes still closed. I had forgotten about having shared the interviews with Mary with her, that she had this in her head as I did in mine.

'I think mine would be the very beginning of being with Andre, the man I thought I was going to marry. Just at that beginning of it all, you know, when all you are doing is getting to know each other and everything is new and interesting and those habits that come to annoy you later all seem endearing. When each day brings a new discovery about the person. You know, that moment when you're making a mental list about the person you are becoming intimate with.'

'Attachment issues,' I said.

Now she was silent.

'Tell me more about that,' she said.

'No, I don't think I will.'

'Just like that? You say: "No, I don't think I will?" Attachment issues? Nothing more? The man who writes twenty-page interviews with warlords and tells everything he sees. They tell you about their sex lives. And you say two words?'

'Intimacy issues. Is that better?'

'Oh yes. Very clear now.'

She did sarcasm well; this amused me. Part of me wanted to share every detail and question that had been going on in my head these last nights, about Sienna, about my confusion, about all that happened with Sienna, and everything left unfinished, about why there was no one else serious since.

'Get close, run away. Women get close. And then I feel this deep-in-my-soul desire to run away or send them away.'

'Stop, you're telling me too much.' she said, and I could imagine the churlish smile that was on her face as she said this.

'Let's just leave it at that for now, okay?' I asked. 'Just pretend that you have extracted a deep secret from me.'

We both reclined in our chairs. The stars became even more brilliant when the last of the lights from the reception and restaurant were turned off. The only light now, besides the stars, was the small nightstand lamp in my room. I crossed my arms over my chest and shivered slightly. I closed my eyes, and while they were closed, Isabelle opened her blanket and spread part of it over me.

'We could just be like the gorillas, no words,' I said. 'Aware of no greater truth than that, just being, eating, grooming … fucking. Or how did our guide put it? Making baby gorillas.'

I paused for a moment.

'Really, would you know me any better if I opened up about my father and how I felt as a boy, and then as a teenager, knowing how he treated women? And how he treated my mother. And how I'm not convinced that I know any better.'

'Know better about what?' she asked.

'About how to treat someone I love or might come to love. How to be in a real relationship. Is that what you want to know?'

Part of me wanted to test her, to see if she would run away, and perhaps to see if we might push the conversation to an edge in which I could ask her about her and Raul.

I sat up and poured us both more wine. We drank in silence and then I returned to my reclining position. We simply sat like that, drinking occasionally and sharing the blanket.

'Yes, I absolutely want to know things like that. I think you would know more about me if you knew that my parents live a fairy tale love story that has been a shadow over the lives of my sisters and me. I think they love each other, but it's so big and so dramatic and the two of them are so … everything. Articulate and elegant and charming without trying.'

She paused for a moment and turned her head away from me.

'All we see is this perfect state all the time. They never show if they have problems or if they have days when they want to push the other one off a roof, which of course they have, because we all have them if we're in a relationship long enough.'

I took a drink and then put my wine glass back on the table. The air was feeling cooler so I slid my hands under the blanket. As I did so, my right hand brushed up against hers.

I left my hand there, just barely touching hers. Without

words, neither of us moved our hands. It felt like the act of a shy fourteen-year-old who is not sure what to do next or if there will be a next. Our stories and words seemed to hover around us like the faintest whiffs of our breath that were becoming visible as the temperature dropped.

There was a slow buildup of current, as if energy needed to jump from one to the other. Our arms were now touching from the back of our hands to our elbows. There was a feeling of static charge where we came in contact.

The first movement of consent, or intent, was turning my hand. My eyes closed, I opened my hand and turned it toward hers and hers crossed over mine. There were no words. Her hand came into mine. At first it was just her closed hand rubbing gently on the inside of mine. Then she moved her hand up to my wrist and up the inside of my forearm.

She began moving it back down to my hand the same way, her fingers lightly touching the inside of my forearm and then, slowly, she fully opened her hand.

Now the inside of her hand was on my forearm, gently sliding down in the direction of my wrist. She lifted her hand slightly at my wrist, letting her fingers slide over it and then her fully opened hand came toward and into mine. I spread my fingers open allowing her fingers to slide gently between them and to come to rest with just the slightest space between our palms.

I cannot recall how long we stayed like that. She put her thumb over mine, slightly rubbing it. She opened her fingers and my hand slid toward my leg so that now I could feel her fingers touching the outside of my thigh. Our hands came in the direction of our thighs, first her hand touching my thigh and then my hand touching hers, feeling the thin cloth of her cotton drawstring pants.

I opened my eyes.

'Isabelle.'

'Shhh,' she said gently. 'No words.'

She sat up slowly, causing the blanket to fall off of us and she turned and gently let herself down onto my chair so she was sitting lightly on my lap. It seemed that her hand had never left mine as she moved. It was if we had an unspoken agreement that we had to leave some part of us touching at all times. As she rested upon me, she reached over and found my other hand and we interlaced those fingers as well, watching our movements and looking at each other in the faint light.

Keeping our hands interlocked, she moved her mouth toward mine, and just as slowly, our lips and tongues met.

The taste in her mouth was thrilling and pleasing and I think we both smiled at the luck of having a kiss be as interesting as we hoped it would be. She was straddling me, and although our bodies were touching, all our energy, for the moment, was there, in this kiss.

She moved her arms around my waist and then I moved mine around her back and up towards her neck and then down again and slightly inside her tank top, just barely touching the skin of her back. She pulled my sweatshirt and T-shirt over my head and put her face to my chest and kissed me and smelled me. Then she pulled off her tank top and guided my hands to her breasts.

Bringing both of her hands to my face she pulled away slowly and stood up and untied her pants, dropping them to the ground and standing in the cool night air in nothing but her underwear. Then, holding my hand, she opened the sliding glass door to my room, and led me inside and closed the door and curtains behind us. With the faint light from the nightstand lamp casting shadows on her body, I removed her underwear and then my jeans and underwear and we touched and smelled and kissed. And she guided me to her.

* * *

'Hey,' I said, early the next morning, running my hand down her back.

'You're still here,' I said.

She turned to me, reaching an arm out cautiously.

'Should I be?' she said.

'We didn't even finish the bottle of wine,' I said.

'No we didn't,' she said.

We were looking at each other, our bodies touching, hands tentatively finding each other, the smell of sex on us and in the bed.

'Should we say more?' she asked and ran her hand down the back of my neck and pulled me to her, kissing me gently on the lips.

She tasted good, strong-smelling but good.

'Maybe. Not now. Later,' I said.

'Later is good,' she said, and kissed me again lightly and got out of bed.

She was as lovely in the light and I think she could feel me watching her get dressed.

'I need to pack my things. See you at breakfast and then we leave after that?' she said.

'Yeah,' I said, with a confused smile.

'What is it?' she asked.

'I was thinking that maybe this was a comfort fuck. But I'd like more comfort.'

She looked at me with a smile that I wanted to wrap up and make mine and mine alone.

'Comfort is good,' she said.

INTERVIEW 4 — MARY OF KIVU

It is always crazy around elections. Eh, it is crazy all the time here, but it waits just beneath the surface. We blame the elections, as if that were the cause. Or we blame the rebels or we blame our neighbors. Eh, we like to blame.

I was telling you about that day. That day my Joseph denied me and I went for a walk in the hills above the clouds where the rebels sometimes hide.

That day, as I walked, I became aware of how quiet it was. At first, it was pleasing, as if it were natural for it to be like that. I could finally think about Edouard and Joseph and all of it. The sadness was alive inside me but I could think clearly now. I hurt inside but I was convincing myself that I would be strong. The quiet gave me strength.

I didn't know that it was the quiet of death and of voices silenced.

I came upon a few simple huts, but I could tell they were abandoned. Some huts and houses were burned down or burned on one side. I knew it was not a natural fire. Suddenly I was very alert.

I could have turned and run. Right then. Perhaps I had a few minutes or even just a minute when I could have run. Maybe I could have gotten away. But I felt myself frozen, as if something made me stand still. Then I heard movement in the bushes and faces appeared—the faces of men carrying guns.

I was silent. I did not greet them with our traditional greeting. They did not greet me. I heard a mumbled word and some grunts and then four or five of them grabbed me at the same time.

They smelled like they had not bathed in many, many weeks. Some of them smelled of alcohol. I was afraid to look in their eyes but I made myself look for a moment, and I could see that their eyes were red and crazed. I wondered if they had taken the drugs that they take to believe that their magic can make bullets turn to water.

The pain that had been turning in my stomach now turned to fear. It felt like I stopped breathing.

In my mind I called out to Joseph.

I knew there was nothing I could say to these men. There was nothing to trade, nothing I could offer that they were not going to take anyway.

My head wrap fell off as they pushed me to the ground. They shouted words to me and to each other. They were calling me 'the pretty one.' I do not remember what else they said.

When I resisted, one of them pulled my arm with such force that I thought he might have broken it. Between the pain of my arm and my clothes being torn off, I thought about the skirt I had ironed again and again in the morning, getting ready to see my Joseph. My Joseph, who had finally come home after four years and turned me away. After I had made myself beautiful for him.

I turned my head from side to side. I cried out. Over and over. *No, no, no, no, no.* I do not remember the moment when they had removed all my clothing.

I do not remember if they had moved me from the clearing and taken me somewhere further into the woods. I think I was dragged. I remember only that my back was stinging and I felt like it was being shredded underneath me.

I don't know if I can tell you how I felt in my body. I was aware of every brutal movement. If one of those *mzungu* women who interview us came with a pad of paper and their questionnaires like they do all the time, I could tell them how many men it was. You *mzungus* always want to know that. *How many times? How many men?*

I don't know why you think that question is important.

'Kill me!' I screamed at them at one point. 'Kill me.'

They laughed at me. My eyes were filled with dust and stinging tears. The pain from that part of my body was so much that I thought I would pass out. I wished I would pass out. I wished to no longer be.

I could not describe any of the men to you. They were stealing from me.

They were taking from me what was mine, the only thing that was truly mine.

When I thought it was over, another was on top of me. Another one grunting and sweating and ripping me apart inside. I thought that I would break into pieces. When the last one got off of me, I was in so much pain that I could hardly even feel relieved that they were done with me. I imagined now that they might kill me. I waited with my eyes closed. I waited for the relief. I hoped only that it would be quick.

I knew the stories. I knew what they did to women after they were done. The things they stuck inside them. Eh, why do they do that? Do we know where that anger comes from? How they can do those things? Do we know?

I prayed they would not do those things. I tried to brace myself for what they might do. I prayed they would just kill me.

As I lay there in the dirt, I could not even make myself close my legs like any decent woman would do. I had no will and no

173

strength. I, who had never been with a man, who wanted so much to be with my Joseph, who was taught that men and women did these things only in the dark, who was taught to be modest except in the quietest of moments with her husband, was spread open on the ground and left like that for anyone to see. For men to see.

I could not understand why they did not kill me. I began to worry that they might take me with them to be a bush wife. That this would happen to me day after day. I prayed with all my energy to die—to be killed.

With all the strength I could find, I opened my eyes and saw the last one with his back to me. He was pulling up his combat pants and had no shirt on. I did not see his face. The only thing I remember as he began walking away was the large scar on his back. It was a scar the shape of Kivu Lake.

I thought my mind was playing tricks on me, or that it was a shadow. It was a shape of something familiar, something that gave me hope, something that made me feel I was still me, that I was still human. That I would live.

My Kivu. Even then, there was my Kivu.

I must have fainted. I don't know how much time passed. I woke up some time later and I wished again I were dead. The first thing I thought was that my family would be angry with me.

'Why were you there?' they would ask. 'What were you doing there?'

I tried to get up but I could not walk at first. There was blood, and I wondered for a moment if they had stabbed me or shot me and left me to die, or if all my woman parts were coming out of me.

I did not want to look at myself. I could not bear to.

I kept trying and eventually I made myself stand up. The pain shot through me and I thought I would fall down. I thought I might have broken ribs. The only way I kept myself standing up was that I imagined they would come back at any time and rape me more.

I could not stop shaking. I made it to the river. I made myself walk along the river's edge. The pain was excruciating. I thought I would fall down at any moment, that I would make it no further and that I would die slowly right here unable to move.

But I kept moving and was able to wash myself in the river. The water was cold and it made me tremble even more. I had managed to pick up my head wrap and I wrapped it around my waist as best I could. I had nothing to cover my top. My bra was torn and was hanging off of me. I shuffled along thinking I would fall again at any moment.

As I walked back the way I had come, I cried. I cried that I had waited for my Joseph. I cried that he had turned me away. I cried for every one of those men who had stolen from me.

I kept walking and crying. I stopped once to drink from the river. I could not stop my hands from shaking, so I had to make myself lean down close to the river and drink like an animal, with my mouth in the water. I can only imagine what I must have looked like, crouched at the water's edge, my back and my women parts still bleeding, my face and arm swollen, tears still streaming down, drinking like an animal, holding my side where my ribs were likely broken.

[Mary stopped speaking for a moment. I was looking at the ground, but I felt her looking at me, as if to tell me that I could look at her, that I must look at her even as she told this. I looked into her eyes and then she turned away from me and calmly continued with her story.]

And then I walked and walked. I would make every single step back to where I started the day. Until I made it to the road and I passed out again and when I woke up I found myself lying on a mat on the ground, in a hut, with a rough pillow under my head.

I looked up and saw the face of the old woman who lived near the falls. I recognized her from the market. She nodded at me with understanding eyes but said nothing. Her look told me that she knew what had happened. It was not a friendly look. There was compassion but, even more, there was anger and disgust.

I wanted to think it was anger at the men who did this to me, but I am not so sure.

She told me to rest, that she would be back in a little while.

I slept for a short time, or better to say that I passed out. I woke up to the sound of a motorcycle. The old woman came in and dressed me in some of her clothes and I heard her saying something to a young man on the motorcycle and I saw her give him money.

'He will take you where they can help you,' she said.

She helped me sit on the motorcycle behind the man and used a wrapper to tie me to the man as if I were a baby on his back.

I was glad this man did not smell like those men. He smelled like my father.

You know the place they took me, Mr. Masterson. The hospital where they help women like me. I am sure you have been. All the *mzungus* go there.

When we got there the man on the motorcycle helped me off and two women from the hospital came to hold me up and then put me on a stretcher and took me inside.

You know, Mr. Masterson, I don't know which is worse. That it happened to me. I mean, when it was happening to me. Or when I was inside the hospital and saw all those women and I thought: *I am just like them. I am one of them now.*

You know what they do there.

They examine you and they listen to you and they do the tests.

They told me I was luckier than some. The damage was not deep. I would not need surgery. I would not have my urine leaking out like some women do. Luckily I was not infected. They told me I could be a normal woman and have a husband, and probably even children.

They said this as if any man would now want me. As if I would just go on with my life. As if I should be happy with this news.

And then they asked me where my family lived and if I wanted to go to them. And they asked me if I was married.

For two days I did not answer the woman who asked me those questions.

'We can talk to your family. We can help you go back home.'

I looked away from her.

Finally I spoke.

'You know how it will be,' I told her.

'We'll talk to them. You should give them a chance. Not all families reject a woman after this has happened.'

'I have no home now,' I told her. 'I have no family.'

She came back the next day and the next day and asked me again and again.

'You can't stay here forever, you know. We need to make space for other women who have experiences like yours. If you don't want to go home, we can help find a village where you can live with other women who have survived experiences like yours.'

Then one day they said I was well enough to leave.

The day I was to leave, they gave me new clothes. There was nothing left of those I had worn that day. The woman and a driver were waiting in a Land Cruiser for me. I got in the car with nothing, nothing in my arms, no bag, nothing but myself, this person I am now.

They waited for me to tell them the name of my village.

I sat there looking straight ahead. I thought about making up a name.

Letting them drive me to some place where no one knew me and telling them to leave me there. And I would get out of the car. And I would find work, find some woman who would take me in to cook for her or some worn-out old man who would marry a woman who had no family to receive the bride price for her and no one to speak on her behalf. Maybe some man who had no family to pay bride price.

And then I told them.

'Ivuko.'

The driver nodded. He looked at me momentarily through the rearview mirror.

'Let's go,' the woman said.

It took nearly a whole day to reach my village. The woman kept asking me questions on the way. She wanted to get me to talk about my family. I sat in silence only telling the driver how to get to my family's house.

It was nearly dusk by the time we arrived. The light at the end of the day made everything seem softer, and I imagined for a moment as we pulled into my village that it might be okay. I saw neighbors sitting in front of their houses. I knew they could recognize the name of the organization on the side of the jeep. I knew they knew what had happened to me and where I had been.

Some of them recognized me through the window of the Land Cruiser. I saw some pointing and saw their gazes follow me. I saw others turn and go into their houses or stores as if they wanted to tell someone else.

And then we reached my house. My father was outside. He was putting away something in the shed where he keeps his tools and things and he looked up at the Land Cruiser and I know he knew it was me.

I told the driver to stop, that I would walk the rest of the way.

My father did not come running to up the car. He just stood watching us, looking at me.

The woman got out of the car to go with me.

'No. Go back to the hospital,' I told her. 'You've done all you can for me and I am grateful. You have others to help.'

'It might be better if we go with you. Jean-Paul can talk to your father and I will talk to your mother.'

'I will talk to them. It is with me now.'

I stood where I was until the woman understood that I was not changing my mind.

And then I walked those thirty meters to my father's house. I could feel his eyes on me. I wanted to believe there was love in them. Or compassion. Maybe there was. But there was something else. Something … something that …

[At this point one of Mary's assistants came in and began whispering in her ear. Mary looked up at me and made a gesture as if to say 'wait.' She stepped out but did not come back. The assistant came in a few minutes later and told me Mary would have to continue the next day.]

THIRTEEN

We arrived back at the guesthouse near Mary's village from the national park around midday. I was sure the staff could see in our eyes that something was different between us. We dropped our things in our respective rooms and then I went to see Mary for the next interview while Isabelle went to her office. We arranged to meet up for dinner in a small place in town that had goat kabobs and reliably cold beer (thanks to a new generator). She didn't suggest including Raul in our dinner plans and we did not see him at the guesthouse.

As I walked out of Mary's house after that interview, after hearing what had happened to her that day in the hills beyond the waterfall, I wanted to leave all of that story locked away in my notes and in my recorder. I wanted to think about other things.

I asked my driver to take me to the Internet café in town. All the messages I had expected were waiting for me. There was one from Sam, one from my mother, and one from Uncle Randall, and some from other researchers and journalists I knew across the area, either sharing what they knew or asking what I knew of the rebel movement.

I wanted to read them all, and yet I would have been happy leaving them unopened. This was one of the privileges of traveling in remote places: I could, for a few days, anyway, leave the world behind. I could have a life somewhere else, continents away, and put it in stasis and focus on this other life, my traveling journalist life. I wanted to think about this unexpected encounter with Isabelle. I wanted to leave the rest behind.

But I could not ignore the message from Uncle Randall.

Dear Keith –

I heard from your mother that you've been hard to reach by e-mail and that because of election violence (I saw it on the news) you've been away from the town where you're working. I am sending this anyway and will also leave a voice mail on your home phone.

I was with your father today when he got the latest test results. They had been trying an aggressive round of combined radiation and chemotherapy, and hoped to see some progress. The news is not good. The cancer has progressed and spread throughout the lung cavity.

I realized what this meant when they sent the social worker to talk to us and she started by saying that it was time to decide how we wanted his last weeks to be.

She said four to six weeks. The doctor couldn't even look us in the eyes and say that. He had to send in the social worker.

I moved him to a hospice today. I have pasted the link below with the phone number and the address.

He wants to see you. I know it would mean a lot to him. He tries to joke in that way of his, tries to convince me to let him smoke and to bring him a bottle of his favorite Balkan wine.

Please call me or let me know that you received this message. And, if you can, try to see him.

Yours,
Randall

I confirmed that I had received the message and I told him to send my love to my father, then I retyped it to say that I sent my father 'warm regards.' I suspected that my uncle might turn that into 'love' anyway.

I was saddened by the news—this confirmation of what I had expected. And yet, compared to Mary's story, and compared to those hours with Isabelle, the news felt like nothing more than the small, descriptive text beneath an intriguing photo.

I sent Sam a quick message that I had resumed my interviews with Mary and was back in easier e-mail range. But before I could see a response from him, the lights flickered and went out. I sat in the dark until the clerk at the Internet café came around with a candle.

'It will come back on soon,' he said.

This was his response every time the power went off, even though I had never seen it come back on in a time frame I would call soon.

I was glad the clerk could not see my face. I paid for the Internet time I had used and walked the dark two blocks to the restaurant. It was earlier than Isabelle and I had agreed upon so I sat down and ordered a beer and pretended to be reading while I stared out across the main street in town. I could hear the restaurant's generator humming in the background.

I was so lost in my thoughts that I did not see Isabelle when she came in the restaurant. I felt her hands on my shoulders and then her mouth lightly at my neck.

'I adore your smell,' she said.

I leaned into her and pulled her to me in a way that gave away my need.

'What's the matter?' she asked.

I told her this latest news about my father.

'I'm so sorry, Keith.'

She leaned over and held my hand for a moment, then looked in my eyes.

'Can I ask you a question that may be difficult to answer?'

I nodded.

'How do you *feel* about it?'

I gave a small laugh.

'Words?' I said.

She held both of my hands.

'There is no sadness, which makes it worse. How do I say this? It's how empty I feel about him that makes me sad. I'd give anything to feel like a little boy who is torn with grief because his father is dying. But instead I feel close to nothing.'

I looked away, letting her hand linger in mine.

'I don't want to see him, lying there in a hospice bed with tubes coming out of him. And it's not because I can't stand that, you know, the body falling apart. It's … it's that I'd stand there with this big hole in front of me, thinking I don't feel a thing for him and I should and I want to and it's his fault that I don't. And then he would die with me telling him that. That would be the last he would hear from me. That I feel nothing for him. Or nothing but anger, anyway.'

'You're talking,' she said, with a warm, silky, understanding voice.

'I'm talking,' I said.

'I hope it's partly because of me.'

'I'm sure it's because of you.'

She held me and I let her. I let my body fall into hers and

I let myself shake with the tears a boy would cry if he had a father he adored and that father were dying. At least some of the tears were because there was someone to see them and to wipe them away.

* * *

Over dinner, we talked about the things that lovers getting to know each other talk about—friends, our favorite trips, what we do when we are home, what we do as soon as we return home after long flights. It was the gathering of information on the other, the compilation of small nothings that we turn into something bigger. There was a flow that was easy and comfortable and I was managing not to feel frightened rolling around in this nest-bed of words with her. And I managed not to think about Mary's story.

We rode back to the guesthouse in my jeep. In the darkness of the car, we held hands and she rested her head on my shoulder.

As we stepped inside the reception area, we were still holding hands and I pulled the memory stick out of my pocket with my other hand.

'You'll want to listen to this,' I said, handing it to her. 'This is the toughest one so far.'

She reached up to touch my face. We both looked up about the same time and saw Raul in the dining room. Our gazes met. Raul nodded in our direction; it was an understanding nod, or at least I took it as such.

'I'm going to my room. I just need to ... Tell Raul I just don't feel like ... '

'It's okay,' she said, before I could finish, and gave me a kiss on the cheek and stroked my hair lightly. 'Knock on my door if you need anything. I mean it.'

I nodded.

* * *

I don't know what time it was when I heard the light knock at my door. It felt very late but I wasn't sure and I did not look at my watch. Isabelle was there in a light gray, jersey-style night-dress.

'Hey, you awake?' she asked.

'Yeah.'

'I listened to it.'

I nodded.

'Hold me,' she said.

She stepped into my room and I closed the door behind her. I put my arms around her.

'Can you hold me for the night?' she asked, looking into my eyes.

I nodded, burying my face in her neck for a moment.

We settled into my bed and both of us fell asleep quickly.

I don't know when it was that I woke up. Lying on our sides, my face to her back, she had pulled my hands around her more closely so they slightly touched her breasts. She moved her hips back into me and then brought her hand up behind her to my face as if to pull my head closer to her.

She brought her hand down my side and then slid it between her hips and mine and reached into my shorts and touched me until I was hard against her.

Then she moved her hand and drew my body into her hips again so she could feel my hardness against her buttocks and on the inside of her thighs. My breath grew hotter at the back of her ear. She turned slightly so she was face down on the bed and opened her legs slightly. First she brought my fingers inside her underwear.

Her face buried in the sheets, she rubbed herself slowly against the bed and against my fingers until she came. Then she pulled off her underwear and lifted herself up on her knees, tilting her hips, waiting for me to put on a condom.

Sometime afterwards, our legs intertwined, she turned to me.

'The first days when I arrived here, when I started doing this research, you know, with women like Mary, I would come back to the guesthouse and cry. Sometimes I would even be ill for a day, as if my body were trying to purge all it had taken in and all I had heard.'

Her accent was especially strong now as she talked softly. She held my face in her hands.

'This way is better.'

* * *

The next morning, I was absolutely sure that I wanted her here with me. I wanted to feel her hand on my face and her breath on my neck. I wanted to have her smell on me and in my bed. I wanted to hear her get up and go to the bathroom and hear the small noises that indicated her presence nearby. In this small, uninspiring guesthouse, I thought this might be that Grecian Urn moment she had asked me about.

INTERVIEW 5 — MARY OF KIVU

So I was telling you about going back home that day I left the hospital. I want you to know this part. I do not know if I will have much more time to meet with you. The next days will be busy. It is not safe here.

Ah, that day still wears on my heart. I walked up to my house with nothing, not even with the clothes I had left home in. My father was watching me but then he turned his back to me once I was up to the house.

'You will bring no bride price now,' he said, with his back turned to me.

That was the first thing he said to me.

'It was not my fault, father.'

'No man will want you now. The village was already talking about how you were seen with both Joseph and Edouard. What will they think now?'

His words were harsh but his voice was soft.

'May I see my mother and my sisters?'

'They are at the neighbors'. They will soon return.'

'May I come into my house and sit down?'

'You can come in but you cannot live here.'

'Father, you can't believe these things they say.'

'You have three sisters who all need husbands. It doesn't matter what I think. The coffee crop was bad this year. We need the bride price. They need to find good husbands. If you are here, no man will call on them.'

He looked at the ground as he said this. He could not look me in the eyes.

'Father ... '

'Go inside. Go. But you cannot stay long. It is not your home anymore.'

He turned away from me and did not go inside with me. He stayed outside by his toolshed, looking as if he had lost something. I know him well enough to believe that he was holding back his tears.

I went inside and sat down and looked around the house. It was as if my father's words had made themselves real. This was not my house anymore. My things—my books, my clothes—were not in the same place. My bed, which had been in the same room with my three sisters, was now in the living room. It was being used as a couch.

I wanted to hate them, to be angry with them, to run away right then. But I knew they could not have known better. They may have thought I was dead, or that I was taken as a bush wife.

I would not let them see me crying when they arrived. I would not.

It was late by the time they came back. I wondered if there had been some way they had known that I was coming home this day, and they had tried to stay out as long as possible. I wondered if they only wanted to be seen with me after it was dark, if somehow word had gotten to them, or if it were just coincidence.

They came in the door saying my name.

'Mary. Mary.'

My mother embraced me and did her best to hold back her tears.

'Oh, why did you go off like that, my daughter?' she said, with more sadness than anger.

'My Mary,' she repeated over and over.

My sisters gave me brief embraces and then looked to the ground. They did not know what to say to me. I could guess what was passing through their heads.

'What will you do?' Adele, my youngest sister, eventually said.

All of us were sitting on the couch that had been my bed. Adele was holding the pillow that had once been mine for sleeping and stroked it on her lap. My mother spoke to me. She could not look into my eyes.

'My daughter, you know we want you to live here with us like before. But you cannot. Your sisters need husbands. You know what the village says about women who … '

She could not finish.

'You know what they say. We want you here but … '

When I was in the hospital, I had gone to a meeting where about ten women with similar experiences to mine told their stories and shared how they tried to get on with their lives. One of the women said that it had been worse to be rejected by her family and her village than it was to have been raped.

I did not believe it when I heard her say that. I did not believe that a family could truly reject a woman after that. At least, I did not believe that mine would. I thought they might just repeat the words they heard in the village. But I did not believe they would really ask me to leave. And I could not believe that whatever my family might do would be worse than being raped.

Now I understood.

'You can sleep here tonight,' my father said. 'But you must leave tomorrow.'

He still could not look into my eyes. I could hear the sadness in his voice even as his words cut into me.

I spread a mat on the floor and tried to sleep. I buried my face in the pillow so they could not hear me cry.

Just before the sun came up, I grabbed several of my books and some of my clothes, all that I could carry in a bag, and I left. I know my mother was awake. I think my father was too. But they said nothing as I quietly walked out the door.

I went to the one place where I thought I would be taken in, the other place that had felt like home these past years. I went to the school.

It was still early when I arrived there. The sun was just beginning to come up.

I found the headmistress in her office.

'My sweet Mary,' she said.

She stood up and came around her desk and hugged me as I had not been hugged since it had all happened.

'I heard what happened,' she said. 'I am so, so sorry, my darling Mary.'

She made me look at her. She could tell I was crying.

'You are strong, Mary. The Lord will help you get through this. I know it.'

I cried more. I cried the tears of relief I had not felt before. I cried the tears of sorrow I had not cried yet. I cried until the morning bell sounded.

'My family … ' I started.

'You can stay here, Mary. This is your home for as long as you need. I just ask one thing of you.'

I looked up at her.

'You will have to teach. Miss Uwera just had her baby and will be out for several weeks, and Miss Mugisha is getting too old to teach all her classes. You will have to work for your keep.'

She smiled at me as she said this, and I managed to smile back at her. I knew what it meant that she would have a woman like me teach at the school. I knew the risk she was taking.

'I will get Sister Irene to prepare a room for you. Today you rest. Tomorrow we'll have you sit in on some classes and review the lesson plans, and then you will begin.'

I knew word would travel fast. I knew word was already traveling, from the moment I had returned to my village. I hoped I would have some weeks, or at least days, before any comments might come from the students or from outside the school. I thought I would have time to talk to the headmistress about what we would do if that happened.

Two days later I started teaching. I was just a few years older than some of the students but with what had happened, and suddenly being made a teacher, I felt as if I were many years older than they were. The headmistress helped me buy some cloth and I had some new wrappers made.

The girls at the school were kind to me. There were a few looks at first but no one said anything. A few said they were sorry to hear about what had happened and one came up to me after class and said: 'Miss Mary, I think you are very brave.'

About two weeks passed and I felt like I knew how to be a teacher. I had to study late into the night to have my lesson plans ready but I felt I was getting better at it. I think the headmistress knew that keeping busy would keep me from thinking all the time about that day, and about Joseph.

The nuns and the other teachers were good to me. I enjoyed seeing all their faces at mealtimes.

Eh, but then the day I thought might come finally came. Judgment day. There was a meeting with parents on a Sunday afternoon and one of the parents brought up my name.

I had not known that I was expected at the meeting. Sister Irene had been sent to summon me. The meeting was in the main dining hall. As I opened the door, I could see that it was full—more than a hundred parents. I heard one father speaking.

'We know that Mary is teaching here. We all know what happened to her. We think it is not right for a woman like her to be teaching our daughters.'

I stood in the doorway and then walked in and sat down on the side of the room where the other teachers were sitting. At first I just stared at the floor. Then I slowly looked around at the faces of the parents.

That's when I saw Joseph's parents. Joseph had a younger sister who was in our school. I saw her occasionally, but she never talked to me and she was not in any of the classes I taught. Then I looked up again and saw Edouard standing with them. Joseph was not with them.

'She cannot be here,' the man continued, casting his eyes in my direction for just an instant.

Then another man stood up and said the same thing.

'We know what happens when a woman like her comes back to her village. She cannot be near our daughters. She may tell them things. Things may happen.'

That man sat down and then Joseph's father stood up.

'You must make her leave. She is not fit to teach here. All of us know that no man would marry her, and for good reason.'

The words hit me like those from my father. Here was my Joseph's father saying this in front of all these people while I had to remain seated and bow my head. I wondered if Joseph and Edouard put him up to this. If they had encouraged him.

For a moment it felt as if all of it was coming back to me—my Joseph sending me away, and those men. I thought my heart could take no more. I thought I might cry out like I did that day and pray to die rather than endure any more.

I thought of running away but I realized I had nowhere else to go. If I was not safe here, I had nowhere else to go.

I could not stop myself from crying. While the tears burned in my eyes, I did not hear the door open behind me. I closed my eyes for a moment.

The headmistress spoke.

'Does anyone have anything else to say about Mary? Do *all* of you agree with this?' she asked.

I could not understand the tone of her words. It was her teacher voice, her lesson voice. I had expected force or anger in her voice. I could not understand why she was asking like this.

After a long silence, there was another voice. This time, the words seemed to come from a dream.

'I will marry her.'

His voice carried through the dining hall. I had never heard it so loud and strong before.

'Even before I went away to university I had planned to marry her. I was confused for a time when I came back. I was angry at her and I would not see her. But I was wrong. I will marry her. I don't care what has happened.'

There was silence for a moment after he said this. I opened my eyes, lifted my head, and turned back to look at him. As I saw his eyes on me, eyes that now looked at me like they once did, I had the feeling that my life and all that I had wanted was coming back to me.

There was grumbling and gasps and words I could not hear and did not try to hear, and then there was silence again. Edouard spoke.

'You are a fool, my brother. You will marry a woman who can't even take care of a sick husband? Who can't care for a child? She is unclean. She cannot touch you. And you don't even know if she carries inside her the seed of a rapist.'

'I am the fool, my brother?' Joseph responded without a pause, his voice still carrying through the room. 'I went to university. I have a degree and a profession.

'I have an education. I have a job. What did you do all these years? Drink and go to parties?'

I so wanted to run to Joseph but I just sat there staring at him.

Then he walked over to me and stood behind me, and put a hand on my shoulder.

'If she will have me, I will marry her. And I will hear nothing against it.

'Anyone here who wants to speak about it can go to the capital and study and see if he can show me in the Bible or in our constitution or anywhere, where it says that a woman who has been raped is unclean. It is silly superstition. Nothing more.'

More was said, I am sure. I do not remember. The headmistress spoke with her headmistress voice and some parents grumbled. Joseph's parents walked out along with Edouard, who stared at me like the devil himself. The other parents stayed for the rest of the meeting, and before long were talking about things like tuition fees and meals and graduation ceremonies.

Joseph stood next to me until the meeting was over then asked if we could go somewhere and talk.

Those first two weeks at the school, I had begun to feel that I was as old as the other teachers and the nuns. I had begun to wonder if I might spend the rest of my life there, growing old together with them.

But after what Joseph said, I felt I was a girl again. My girl's heart had been given back to me.

Joseph took my hand and as we walked out the doors of the dining hall, I felt as if now, finally, my life had begun.

There was much more, of course. Much more to come. Redemption always has a price. Eh, Mr. Masterson? And, as the headmistress says, the bigger the redemption, the higher the price.

FOURTEEN

Mary turned to me, as if she were going to tell me more, but then looked at me intensely, as if searching inside me or asking something of me. I reached down and turned off the recorder. I put my pen and notebook down. She smiled at me as I did this, as if she knew I would do this and what would happen next. She spoke in English.

'Mr. Masterson, we have always been talking about me. You journalists. And you men. You don't talk about what is happening inside you.'

She nodded in the direction of the translator, who promptly stood up and left us alone.

Mary let the silence sit in the room. It was the first time in all the interviews that there was silence. She had, up until now, talked without my prompting. She remembered where we had left off from the interview before and she kept talking until each interview ended, an hour or two later. But now she let the silence sit with us.

I felt it as a cloud engulfing me, a cloud that I was sure Mary could see and one that, if she had wanted to, she could have waved away with a slight movement of her hand.

It was a silence that carried the weight of all the interviews I had done these past years without ever talking about myself. I was the *mzungu* with no past and no family or village they could connect me to, with no connection to any of this, with no connection to them. I was the *mzungu* listening to and probing the pasts of men and women as if they were merely stories, as if lives could be poured into articles and I could move on to the next one and the next one.

I had listened to stories of rape, of children killed. I had listened to genocide survivors recounting the last words they would ever hear from their parents or their spouses, to warlords who ordered rape and who sometimes showed remorse but who more often wanted to tell me about their families, to colonels who asked for my advice about their daughters and invited me into their houses and showed me pictures of the children and wives they had left behind in the capital and hadn't seen for years, to women on the side of the road who had just been raped and had their children abducted. And this: to women rejected by their families whom I asked how they felt about it, and when I asked what they would do with their lives after this they never told me that that was the stupidest question they had ever heard.

I would look into their eyes and I would nod. Then I would look down to my recorder, making sure the red recording light was on and I would glance at my notebook, making a mental note of a detail that I would later use.

And when it was over I would thank them and go back to my jeep, and nod to my driver to leave, and I would wave as we drove away and headed back to wherever we had started the day, and I would spend hours typing up the words and details of their lives and later press *upload attachment* and *send* and think nothing of rendering all they had lived and suffered into electronic streams that ended up read by *mzungus* sitting safely in their living rooms, somewhere far away from all of this.

I believed that Mary understood this, that she saw this, that she could perceive me thinking this. I smiled back at her as I realized that this was obvious to her and to Isabelle and perhaps to every man or woman I had interviewed all these years.

I remembered then that Mary had smiled gently at me when I said I wanted two hours to interview her, as if she or any of these lives could be known.

Finally, I spoke.

'You know about my father but I don't know how,' I said.

'Does it matter how I know?' she asked.

I shook my head.

'And I think you must know much more about me,' I said.

She looked at me patiently, neither confirming nor denying this.

'That woman who was with you when you came the first day. There is something between you, isn't there?' she asked. 'Maybe you are in love with her.'

I nodded.

And then I talked. I don't know how long I talked. Maybe it was an hour, perhaps longer. I talked about my father, about his famous photograph, about his illness, about my mother, about what I do for a living, about the stories I gather, about the doubts about the stories I gather, about Sienna, about Isabelle. About how much Isabelle already meant to me and about the feeling that it could all come tumbling down with her and that for the first time in my life I had no idea what I would do if it did.

Mary simply listened to it all, nodding occasionally, and looking at me with her soft yet penetrating gaze.

As I finished, I looked her in the eyes. I had the feeling that if she touched me, so much as rested a hand on my arm, I might crumble into a million pieces, into a *me* beyond recognition. I know she could see this.

She reached over and touched my arm.

'See, Mr. Masterson, you are still here.'

Then she continued, as if we had never stopped the interview, as if I had paid at least part of what I owed her, and as if there was something else she wanted me to know before our session ended.

'I didn't tell you about the wedding and about my life now, I think. You see, my Joseph proposed that we wait to have the wedding until the semester finished at my school. That would give him time to build a house near the tea plantation, a house fit for a tea plantation manager and his family. He would not have me living in his parents' house.

'Are you following me, Mr. Masterson?'

I nodded.

'I agreed to it all on the condition that he come to see me every day after he got off work and that he take me to see the house. You see, I wanted a courtship like any girl wants. And I asked my Joseph to negotiate the bride price with my father. That goes with the courtship here. He agreed to all those things and the date was set for our wedding.

'It was held in the chapel at the school and Father Ningonwe performed the ceremony. The headmistress was my maid of honor. I think you know her. After the ceremony, we took a weekend on Lake Kivu and my Joseph hired a boat and driver. We talked and held hands while we toured the islands as we had all those years ago. Only now we could go as husband and wife with all the time we wanted, without hiding from anyone.

'And then we moved into this house where we sit now.'

I nodded.

'Make sure you get this next part, Mr. Masterson.'

Again she paused.

'I am sure you want to know if we are husband and wife like any normal couple. If I am able to enjoy relations with my husband. *Mzungus* always want to know that.'

I stared at her.

'He loves me, Mr. Masterson. My Joseph loves me in all the ways a woman wants and needs to be loved.'

I nodded. She shifted slightly in her chair as if she was about to stand up, as if to signal that the interview was ending.

'But *you* are still not telling me something,' she said.

'You know, then?' I asked.

'It is you who must know.'

She reached over and touched my arm.

'It is you who needs forgiveness, Mr. Masterson.'

I remained in silence. With her eyes she told me she did not expect me to reply.

'Come back tomorrow,' she told me. 'I don't know if it will be possible, but I will try to find time to tell you the rest. There is still more you must know. You must know about my son.'

I stood up to leave.

'You must tell her,' Mary told me as I was picking up my recorder and my notebook. 'She deserves to know.'

'I know,' I said. 'I know.'

FIFTEEN

Isabelle was sitting outside at a table in the small garden behind our guesthouse. There was a partial view from there of the hills around us. It was lush green this time of year, just a few weeks after the end of the rainy season. It was the time of the coffee harvest.

Two small children, evidently the son and daughter of one of the staff at the guesthouse, were playing in the garden. I remembered having seen them once before through the door to the kitchen. Isabelle saw me as I stopped to greet the children, leaning down to shake hands with them. I saw the boy's eyes light up. Moving slowly towards him and making sure he wasn't frightened of me, I picked him up and threw him into the air and then did the same with the girl when she asked me in Swahili to toss her as well. Then they did what young children everywhere do: they asked me to do it again, and again. It was only when their mother came out and called them inside that I stopped.

Isabelle was smiling at me.

'Hi,' she said. 'You're back early.'

'I wanted to see you.'

'You want to go for a walk?' she asked.

'Sure.'

We walked on a trail that connected to the main road and ran behind our guesthouse, eventually reaching Mary's school.

It was pleasant at the end of the day. The few people we saw on the trail greeted us in Swahili or French, but mostly we were ignored.

We walked in silence for a few minutes. It felt like the good silence of a couple that can be content just to walk and be together without always needing words.

'Children adore you,' she said, taking my hand.

She paused; I could sense she wanted to ask me something.

'May I ask?' she said, looking at me with a mischievous smile.

I looked on, puzzled; she continued.

'Do you want to have children someday?'

I looked at the horizon, wishing I could put that question back where it came from, or believing that if I stayed quiet long enough she would forget she had asked it and I could forget what Mary had told me that I must do.

'Is that too intimate a question for the moment?' she asked, when I did not answer.

This is how it comes tumbling down. This is where I run away. This is when I run from the little girl who followed me when I was running in the village that day. This is where I outpace her and leave her behind and never look back.

'Keith? What is it?'

Nothing. Nothing. Nothing.

'Nothing,' I finally said.

It sounded aggressive.

I stopped and rubbed my hands on my face.

'What is it? Please tell me.'

Nothing. Nothing. Nothing.

Then I looked at her.

'I have a child. A daughter. She's in the US.'

I stopped before saying more. I could see the effect of the words on Isabelle.

She turned away from me. She pulled her hand away from mine.

'She must be four, almost five, by now. She lives with her mother in Wisconsin. At least I think they're still there. I've never met her.'

Again, Isabelle looked at me blankly, saying nothing, trying to make sense of this. I wondered if she might turn and run away, or if she had a string of curses to hurl at me.

'I'm listening,' she said.

'Sienna, her mother, was my girlfriend in graduate school.'

I leaned against a fence that bordered one side of the trail.

'She's a lovely person. I loved her, although I didn't want to admit it. We started going out right after her older sister died in childbirth.

'It explains a lot. Why she wanted to have a baby no matter what. And why it didn't matter what I thought. Maybe why she liked me in the first place. She said I was good with children.'

I stopped and looked at Isabelle. She was staring at the ground.

'And she wanted the child,' Isabelle said.

'She wanted the child,' I echoed.

'I was planning to break up with her. I mean, I did break up with her.

'Before we knew that she was pregnant. I didn't want to be that close to her. Or maybe I did. Maybe I loved her. I was afraid and I was confused and I had plans to come here, to write my book, to travel to Africa. This is what I wanted to do more than anything else.'

'No reason to get close to anyone,' Isabelle said, cynicism creeping in to her voice.

Then she continued.

'But how can you *not* have any contact with her, your daughter, or not be curious. I can't imagine … '

'I am curious, it's just … ' I said.

Now she crossed her arms in front of her and rubbed them as if she had a chill.

'Does the mother, I mean Sienna, refuse to let you see your daughter?'

'No, she didn't refuse. It's just that the deal we made was that she would raise her alone and I wouldn't have any contact.'

'But you agreed not to have any contact?'

Her voice was becoming tense, her accent stronger.

'No, it wasn't like she made me swear I would never contact her. But she knew I wouldn't.'

I stopped for a moment.

'Yes. Yes. I chose not to be in contact. She chose to be a single mother.'

'I mean, I understand that you were against it. But she had the child. How could you not want to see your child? To have her know you … '

'Women decide all the time to have children without men. That's what she said she wanted.'

'But you … *you* could go meet your daughter. That's your decision, not hers. Why wouldn't you go see her?'

I did not respond. I was looking at the highway. I was watching the families returning from the market and from their day's work. Women with babies on their backs. Men with tools over their shoulders. Children in school uniforms carrying backpacks over their shoulders. A bus laden with people and packages inside and bundles on top, spewing black smoke as it pushed up a hill. I was remembering the day Sienna told me she was pregnant. I was looking for an emergency escape from my own head.

'What's your daughter's name?' Isabelle eventually said.

'Eliza.'

I turned to look at her.

'Sienna's sister was named Elizabeth. She said there's a piece of Elizabeth in her.'

I wanted to say that that didn't matter, that it was maudlin to name her that.

I wanted to say anything that would bring Isabelle back to where we were just minutes before.

'I have work to do,' Isabelle said. 'I need to get back to the guesthouse.'

She turned to look me in the eyes.

'Keith, I have to think about what all this means.'

She turned and began walking back to the guesthouse at a pace that told me she did not want me to follow her.

INTERVIEW 6 — MARY OF KIVU

I am glad you could come today. Eh, those men don't stop coming. First the rebels come with hate in their hearts, their minds all crazy from the drugs they take. And then, when we finally have some calm, the other men decide they must get their revenge. This hate is like a devil that feeds on its own tail. They said they would be back today with more proof and that they would not leave empty-handed.

They want my houseboy. Do you know him? Franklin?

I will tell you about him. But first, you must know about my son.

You see, Mr. Masterson, I found out I was pregnant just a few weeks before our wedding. It was on the day Joseph was showing me this house. It was almost completed. Everyone says it is the nicest in the village. I told Joseph to make it simple. But he wanted to have a house that was nice enough for a tea plantation manager and his family. That's what he always said when he was having it built.

Joseph and my father agreed on a bride price. Eh, my Joseph insisted on paying more than my father had asked for. I think he wanted to make a point that I was as valuable as any woman in the village. The *most* valuable one, he said.

As I looked at the house that day, Joseph could tell that something was on my mind. So I looked him in the eyes and I told him.

'I am pregnant.'

He knew without asking that it was from that day, from one of those men.

He turned away and looked out the kitchen window that looked onto the hills full of tea bushes and then he spoke.

'I will raise it, and name it and love it as my own. We will say nothing more of it.'

And so less than six months after our wedding, I gave birth to our son. He is perfectly healthy and my Joseph has honored his word. He loves our son as a father should love a child. He has never said a word to the contrary.

We had a house girl with me from the beginning. But with this garden, and with what had happened, I liked the idea of a man around while Joseph was at work. So my Joseph went over to the area near the docks by the lake, you know, the place where they wash cars and motorcycles, near where the ferries dock. There are always young men there looking for work.

He knew a young man, very quiet, who always washed the vehicles for the tea plantation.

'I will go find that boy,' he said. 'He seems trustworthy. It's good to have someone from outside the village who won't gossip or cause any problems.'

A few days later he brought Franklin to live with us to be the houseboy, to work in the garden and to be our guard if we needed it, to have a man around even though Joseph was close by at the estate office.

It was when Franklin came to live with us that my gift, this gift that brings those lines of people outside, came to me.

I could look at Franklin and tell things about him, things he had done or might do. I don't know how to explain it. I could tell he was troubled. Don't ask me how, but I knew he had been with the rebels. I could see things in his eyes that he had done.

And then one day he started shaking. Trembling. I didn't know what it was. Memories? The spirits of those he had killed? Epilepsy? I don't know. I touched his shoulder and wiped his face dry of sweat and the moment I touched him he stopped shaking.

I thought it was nothing. But the housegirl was there too and the neighbor had come over. They all saw it.

The next day, the neighbor brought her mother. Her mother also had a kind of shake, and she could barely walk. I said that I didn't do anything, I just wiped Franklin's forehead. But my neighbor insisted that I do the same for her mother.

I kept saying that nothing would happen, that I didn't do anything special but she kept insisting.

So I took a cloth and wiped her mother's forehead. And just like with Franklin, my neighbor's mother stopped shaking. Her eyes took on a shine that they hadn't had for years and she was able to walk nearly upright again.

I didn't believe it. I didn't believe that I did anything unusual.

Eh, but word travels faster than sunshine in our village, and the next day more people came. And the same thing happened. I insisted that I had no special abilities and they insisted only that I wipe the foreheads of their loved ones. Every time, the person got better. They weren't always healed completely but they always improved.

Within a few weeks, it turned into this.

I still don't know how it happens or why. I wipe their foreheads with a little water and it happens.

Eh, Mr. Masterson, I am tired after all these months. But if it is true, if I am really healing them, then I must carry on. It is my duty.

With the blessing comes that curse. And another one.

You see, word got out that Franklin had been with the rebels. And now the men with revenge in their hearts want to take him away. I know they will kill him if they take him.

My poor Franklin cannot live with this weight on this heart and so that day, I think you remember, he tried to set himself on fire.

You know, Mr. Masterson, that is the same thing they did to his family. The rebels. They made him watch while they burned his family alive.

So when he tried to kill himself that day, I pulled him out of the fire. Even so, those men who want revenge keep coming back. Today they have promised to bring proof of what he has done. They have threatened to take him away and they say that no one will stop them. Not even the soldiers or the police. They talk their big talk.

But as the Lord guides me, it won't happen today.

I don't know what will happen tomorrow.

I don't know what they would do if they knew that my darling son is the child of a rebel like Franklin. But as long as I am here, they will harm no one.

[Mary stopped. She lifted her head as if she could hear something, although I had heard nothing unusual. Then one of her assistants came in and said: 'Those men are back. There are more of them today. They have pangas. They may have guns. They have a woman with them who says she knows what Franklin did. And there are two police with them. They say they want to see you.']

SIXTEEN

As Mary stood up to follow her assistant out the door, she reached out and touched my arm.

'Be strong, Mr. Masterson. You know what you must do.'

As she walked out of the room, I could hear the voices. There was shouting and the sound of a crowd gathering. I quickly packed my backpack, closed my notebook and checked my digital recorder to make sure I had captured this last interview and then I went outside.

In front of the house, there were now several vehicles parked, and, as the assistant said, there were some twenty men with *pangas*, with two policemen next to them. A woman stood next to one of the policemen.

Behind them all, farther from the house, were all those who had been waiting in line. There must have been at least three hundred people.

I came out of the house and, not sure where to stand, moved to one side where I could see the crowd but was not directly in their line of movement. My driver saw me and walked quickly to where I was.

'We should leave,' he said. 'It is not safe.'

'No, I want to stay. Tell me what they're saying.'

He looked at me for a moment and, seeing that I would not change my mind, he explained that one of the men with a *panga* said that the woman next to them had been raped by Franklin.

'Tell them what happened,' the man with the *panga* said to the woman.

She described the day they came. They raped her and took her as a bush wife. Franklin was one of her bush husbands. She knew his real name because he had told her and he told her the name of his village.

There was movement and noise from the crowd.

'Bring out your houseboy Franklin,' the head man with the *panga* said.

Mary stepped away from her house and spoke.

'He will come outside as you ask, but you will not harm him. And you will not take him away.'

'*We* will decide what happens to him,' the head man with the *panga* said.

One of Mary's assistants stepped inside the house and Franklin came out a moment later. Mary stood next to him.

'Is this the man who was your bush husband?' the head man with the *panga* asked the woman next to him.

'That is him,' she said.

Mary took a step out in front of Franklin, moving closer to the men with *pangas*. Franklin looked at the ground, his shoulders sagging. He wore the simple beige uniform of a houseboy.

'Do you know what happened to this man? Do any of you know?' Mary shouted, holding her head erect.

I had not imagined her voice carrying like this, the force in it.

'He was made to rape his sister. His ten-year-old sister. If he did not, they said they would rape and kill his mother in front of him and then kill him and all his family. Can any of you imagine that? Who here knows what that is like? Who here can say your heart would not harden if you had to do that?

'This is what the rebels do to make men like Franklin into killers. These things are shameful to our culture. Making grown men have sex with their mothers and sisters or forcing them to watch as their mothers and wives are raped. We are not supposed to even see our mothers like that, let alone be made to do that to them. Do you know how this hardens men's hearts?

'And do you know that even though he did what they said, they killed everyone in his family except for him? They put his family into their house and poured gasoline on it, and they held Franklin's hand and made him light the match. Do any of you what that is like?

'He became one of them. There was nothing else for him to do.'

The crowd was quiet, staring at Mary as she spoke.

'I was raped by many men one day. I was so overcome that I could not look at their faces. The only thing I remember is that the very last man who raped me had a scar on his back that that was the exact shape of our Lake Kivu. I thought I was delirious. A scar the shape of Lake Kivu. That is all I remember of those men. But I know that I saw it.'

Mary turned and looked at Franklin.

'Franklin, would you take off your shirt? No one will hurt you, I promise you.'

The houseboy looked up with fear in his eyes.

'Please,' Mary said, her voice understanding but forceful.

Franklin slowly removed his shirt but left his back facing away from us.

215

'Turn your back to us please.'

He turned his back slowly to the crowd and there was a collective gasp.

There on his back was a scar that was, as Mary described, a large keloid in the shape of Lake Kivu. It looked like it could have been caused by a *panga* wound or perhaps by a burn.

'Franklin was one of those men who robbed me of my honor that day. And he may have been one of the men who raped you too, my sister,' Mary said, looking at the woman. 'I did not know who he was when he came to work for us. But I saw his scar one day when he was working in our garden and I knew. I did not tell my husband. I did not tell anyone. I did not tell Franklin. He did not recognize me. But now you all know.'

Mary moved a step back so she was standing next to Franklin again. He was looking down at the ground, avoiding our eyes and holding one hand up to his face and rubbing it as if he thought he could wipe away his features.

'He is welcome in our house as are any and all who bring love and contrition in their hearts.'

There was silence and then shouts that my driver did not translate.

'You will not take him. Not today. He is a repentant man. And for repentant men, we leave it to God to decide their fate.'

The next few moments are vague for me. I saw things and then again maybe I didn't see anything unusual. It was early evening, approaching dusk, and the sun was beginning to dip low in the sky; it was the time of day that filmmakers and photographers adore. Shadows were accentuated and angles elongated. My father used to point this out to me.

I saw a man on the porch behind Mary. He was holding a child, a small boy, and I knew it had to be Joseph. I wondered if he had been there before and I simply had not noticed. He looked on calmly. If he was surprised by any of this, he did not show it. It was the first time I had ever seen him. He was tall, with gentle features; he held his head high and had a calm and confident look on his face. He wore a neatly pressed short-sleeved white shirt with *guayabera*-style pockets on the front. About those details, I am sure.

About this next part, I'm not sure. I was pushed out of the way by my driver, who was trying to keep me safe, and I saw things only through rows of people in front of me.

What I think I saw was light. Pure light. It was brighter than the natural light falling at the end of the day and I have trouble giving it much more form or substance than that. I do know it was an unusual light.

My theory about these things is this: when we see this light, this light we can't quite describe, but we feel it and know it is there, we give it a face. We need it to be an image that we can identify in our heads so that we can describe it to others and so that it makes sense to us. For most of us, it represents love in its purest form. For those from villages like Mary's, indoctrinated by a series of images said to represent this, the apparitions they describe are well known. Everyone has seen the shrines they build afterwards.

But I had no such image to draw on.

As the crowd moved in ways and directions that made no sense, and as *pangas* swung violently but met no objects and cut into no flesh, I saw only Mary Kirezi of Kivu and next to her, glowing in that unusual light, Joseph Kirezi of Kivu, holding a child in his arms.

LIGHT GETS IN

When I returned to the guesthouse that evening, Raul was alone in the dining room. Even before he spoke, I had an idea of what he would say. I had the feeling that she was not there. I could not feel her presence.

'Hey.'

'Hey.'

'Isabelle asked me to tell you that she had to travel to Kinshasa to meet with one of their big funders. She doesn't think she'll be back here before she returns to Geneva.'

I shook my head and looked away from him.

'She told me a little of what you told her.'

'Yeah,' I said in the tone of a seventeen-year-old version of myself.

'Yeah,' he said back, echoing my tone.

'Isabelle asked me to give you this,' he said, handing me a small envelope.

'Thanks,' I said.

'Hey, if you want to have dinner, have a beer, talk about this or not talk about this, let me know. I'll be here for a few more days at least,' he said.

He waited for me to respond but I did not.

'I heard that some interesting things just happened at Mary's house,' he continued. 'I suppose I will have to investigate.'

I nodded.

'Yeah, you should investigate,' I said. 'Thanks, um, right now I just need to pack and … think.'

'Sure,' he said.

* * *

I went to my room and opened the envelope from Isabelle. There was the memory stick I had given her and a CD. There was a note taped to the CD.

> Dear Keith: Play track 2. It is the song I told you about the other night. I believe it and I think you do too. I truly enjoyed our time together. It was special to me, as are you. Someday, I believe you'll use your words to mend the things that need to be mended. Yours, Isabelle.

On the other side of the CD she had taped her business card. Written at the bottom of that, she had put her home telephone number.

* * *

Track 2 was the Leonard Cohen song, 'Anthem.' I had somehow missed this in my musical education. I could vaguely recall some of his songs, mostly the ones sung by others, but his voice had never captivated me and his lyrics had always struck me as too cumbersome.

Of course Isabelle would like these overwrought lyrics, and of course this endeared her to me. I listened to it three or four times as I packed my bags to return to New York.

... the wars they will
be fought again
The holy dove
She will be caught again ...

Ring the bells that still can ring
Forget your perfect offering
There is a crack in everything
That's how the light gets in.

* * *

My father died when I was in route thirty-plus hours back to New York City from Lake Kivu. I found out after I landed.

There was a message from Randall on my mobile phone and on the answering machine in my apartment, and one from my mother.

'We thought he would last longer,' Randall said in the message. 'The funeral will be next Saturday. I heard from your mother that you should be back today.'

He left me the address of where the funeral would be, near Princeton, New Jersey, where my father had been living the past few years. He taught a seminar on journalism and public policy at Princeton and worked free-lance for one of the major photo agencies.

My uncle had arranged the ceremony; it was in a seminar room at a small hotel near campus. He had managed to book rooms for most of the family members. He brought my grandparents from Ithaca; while both are in good health, they do not like to drive long distances by themselves.

It was good to see them all, and the mood of the ceremony meant that I did not have to explain why I was distant and morose-looking. I think some of them took it as a sign of generosity that I showed so much apparent sadness about my father.

There were colleagues of his who said some words about what he had meant to the profession. There were photos of his on easels and a thoughtful obituary in the *Times* and one in *The Economist* that referenced his famous photo; political analysts of the Balkans wars affirmed again that the photo had been part of convincing NATO to finally take a stand. There were compliments on my book on the Lord's Resistance Army and the inevitable comments about me following in his line of work. And every time someone asked that question that we always get—*What are you working on now?*—I steered the conversation to my interviews with Mai Mai commanders. I could not talk about Mary of Kivu.

* * *

For three days after the funeral I did not answer the phone or respond to e-mails. I spent the days writing up and editing my notes from the interviews with Mary. On the day I finished writing them up, I was preparing to call Sam and send him all that I had written.

Instead I called some former classmates and found Sienna's current telephone number.

Her voice was cautious; she responded with long pauses, but I could not detect anger. I imagined her face; I tried to picture it slightly older, her red hair, her generous smile, her fierce gaze.

She had seen the news about my father and asked me to give my family her condolences.

'She's four now, turns five the end of May,' Sienna said. 'Four and gotten used to not having a father.'

'What have you told her?' I asked.

'That some fathers choose not to be with their children, or can't be with their children, and that some fathers are not ready to be fathers.'

'Sienna, I'd like to see her. Not just see her, but be in her life somehow.'

'Keith, you know she's not six months old. She's four, nearly five as she likes to remind me, and making sense of the world and choosing things for herself. We have to ask her if she wants to see you.'

'Okay.'

'And I want to think about how I'll tell her.'

'Okay.'

'It might not be tomorrow. And she might say she doesn't want to see you at first. Right away. You have to be prepared for that.'

'Yeah, okay.'

Before I hung up, I made sure that Sienna had all my phone numbers and my e-mail and that she had my mother's number as well. I wanted to make sure she could find me—that my daughter could find me.

As I hung up the phone, I thought: Of course I will wait. Where else would I be going? And then I decided this: I will write this story, about Mary and Joseph, for my daughter. It will be for Eliza, whenever she is ready.

The Democratic Republic of Congo portrayed here is both very real and at the same time completely out of my head. Mary and Joseph are mythical and yet I hope they breathe with the voices of women and men from the region— people whose lives are richer and more powerful than I could possibly convey here. For her inspiration, insights, and ruthlessly ethical advocacy on behalf of DR Congo, Burundi, and Rwanda, I thank my friend and colleague Henny Slegh. Thanks also to Augustin Kimonyo, Benoit Ruratotoye, Oswald Mwizwerwa, and Fidele Rutayisire. For believing in this story and for gentle guidance along the way, my special thanks to Eric Visser. Thanks as well to Ann Patty for her brilliant eye for storytelling and her razor-sharp attention to detail.

For their support and encouragement as I insist on making fiction out of my day job—and for reading my work before it's ready for the world—my deepest thanks to Michael Kaufman, Madeline Wilks, Alyse Bass, Niobe Way, Simone Ratzik, Michael Kimmel, Tatiana Moura, and Robert and Phyllis Barker.

Finally, I thank my daughter, Nina, and my partner, Suyanna Linhales Barker, for bringing the light, and for everything else.